BUNNY BROWN AND HIS SISTER
SUE KEEPING STORE

BY

LAURA LEE HOPE

CHAPTER I

A GRAND CRASH

Patter, patter, patter came the rain drops, not only on the roof, but all over, out of doors, splashing here and there, making little fountains in every mud puddle.

Bunny Brown and his sister Sue stood with their faces pressed against the windows, looking out into the summer storm.

"I can make my nose flatter'n you can!" suddenly exclaimed Bunny.

"Oh, you cannot!" disputed Sue. "Look at mine!"

She thrust her nose against the pane of glass so hard that it almost cracked—I mean the glass nearly cracked.

"Look at that, Bunny Brown!" exclaimed Sue. "Isn't my nose flatter'n yours? Look at it!"

"How can I look at your nose when I'm looking at mine?" asked Bunny.

He, too, had pushed his nose against the glass of his window, the children standing in the dining room where two large windows gave them a good view of things outside.

"You must look at my nose to see if it's flatter'n yours!" insisted Sue. "Else how you going to know who beats?"

"Well, I can make mine a flatter nose than yours!" declared Bunny. "You look at mine first and then I'll look at yours."

This seemed a fair way of playing the game, Sue thought. She left her window and went over to her brother's side. The rain seemed to come down harder than ever. If the children had any idea of being allowed to go out and play in it, even with rubber boots and rain coats, they had about given up that plan. Mrs. Brown had been begged, more than once, to let Bunny and Sue go out, but she had shaken her head with a gentle smile. And when their mother smiled that way the children knew she meant what she said.

"Now, go ahead, Bunny Brown!" called Sue. "Let's see you make a flat nose!"

Bunny drew his face back from the window. His little nose was quite white where he had pressed it—white because he had kept nearly all the blood from flowing into it. But soon his little "smeller," as sometimes Bunny's father called his nose, began to get red again. Bunny began to rub it.

"What you doing?" Sue wanted to know, thinking her brother might not be playing fair in this little game.

"I'm rubbing my nose," Bunny answered.

"Yes, I know. But what for?"

"'Cause it's cold. If I'm going to make my nose flatter'n yours I have to warm it a little. The glass is cold!"

"Yes, it is a little cold," agreed Sue. "Well, go ahead now; let's see you flat your nose!"

Bunny took a long breath. He then pressed his nose so hard against the glass that tears came into his eyes. But he didn't want Sue to see them. And he wouldn't admit that he was crying, which he really wasn't doing.

"Look at me now! Look at me!" cried Bunny, talking as though he had a very bad cold in his head.

Sue took a look.

"Yes, it is flat!" she agreed. "But I can flatter mine more'n that! You watch me!"

Sue ran to her window. She made up her mind to beat her brother at this game. Closing her teeth firmly, as she always did when she was going to jump rope more times than some other girl, Sue fairly banged her nose against the window pane.

Her little nose certainly flattened out, but whether more so than Bunny's was never discovered. For Sue banged herself harder than she had meant to, and a moment later she gave a cry of pain, turned away from the window, and burst into tears.

"What's the matter?" asked Mrs. Brown, hurrying in from the next room: "Who's hurt?"

Sue was crying so hard that she could not answer, and Bunny was too surprised to say anything for the moment. Mrs. Brown looked at the two children. She saw Sue holding her nose in one hand, while Bunny's nose was turning from white to red as the blood came back into it.

"Have you children been bumping noses again?" she asked. This was a game Bunny and Sue sometimes played, though they had been told not to.

"No, Mother; we weren't 'zactly banging noses," explained Bunny. "We were just seeing who could make the flattest one on the window, and Sue bumped her nose too hard. I didn't do anything!"

"No, it—it wasn't Bun—Bunny's fault!" sobbed Sue. "I did it myself! I was trying to—to flatter my nose more'n his!"

"You shouldn't play such games," said Mother Brown. "I'm sorry, Sue! Let me see! Is your nose bleeding?" and she gently took the little girl's hand down.

"Is—is—it?" asked Sue herself, stopping her sobs long enough to find out if anything more than a bump had taken place.

"No, it isn't bleeding," said Mrs. Brown. "Now be good children. You can't go out in the rain, so don't ask it. Play something else, can't you?"

"Could we play store?" asked Bunny, with a sudden idea. It was not altogether new, as often before, on other rainy days, he and Sue had done this.

"Oh, yes, let's keep store!" cried Sue, forgetting all about her bumped nose.

"That will be nice," said Mother Brown. "Tell Mary to let you have some things with which to play store. You may play in the kitchen, as Mary is working upstairs now."

"Oh, now we'll have fun!" cried Sue, clapping her hands.

"Could we have Splash in?" asked Bunny.

"The dog? Why do you want him?" asked Mrs. Brown.

"We could tie a basket around his neck," explained Bunny, "and he could be the grocery delivery dog!"

"Oh, yes!" laughed Sue.

"No," said Mother Brown, with a gentle shake of her head, "you can't have Splash in now. He has been splashing through mud puddles and he'd soil the clean kitchen floor. Play store without Splash."

There was one nice thing about Bunny Brown and his sister Sue. If they couldn't have one thing they did very well with something else. So now Bunny said:

"Oh, all right! We can take turns sending the things out ourselves, Sue."

"Yes, and we'll take turns tending store," added Sue. "'Cause I don't want to be doing the buying all the while."

"Yes, we'll take turns," agreed Bunny.

Soon the children were in the kitchen, keeping store with different things from the pantry that Mary, the cook, gave them to play with. Unopened boxes of cinnamon, cloves and other spices; some cakes of soap in their wrappers just as they had come from the real store, a few nuts, some coffee beans, other beans, dried peas and a bunch of vegetables made up most of the things with which the children played. After they had finished their fun everything could be put back in the pantry.

Bunny tore some old newspapers into squares to use in wrapping the "groceries." Mary also gave the children bits of string for tying bundles.

The store counter was the ironing board placed across the seats of two chairs in front of a table, and on the table back of this ironing board counter the different things to sell were placed.

"What are we going to do for money?" asked Bunny, when the "store" was almost ready to open.

"I'll give you some buttons," said his mother.

Bunny was given a handful of flat buttons of different sizes and colors to use for change. He placed them in his cash box. Sue also had other buttons to use as money in buying groceries.

"Now we're all ready to play," said Bunny, looking over the store. "You must come and buy something, Sue."

"Yes. And then I want to keep store," said the little girl.

"All right," her brother agreed.

Bunny took his place behind the counter and waited. Sue went out into the hall, paused a moment, and then, with a little basket over her arm, came walking in, as much like a grown-up lady as she could manage.

"Good morning, Mrs. Snifkins!" exclaimed Bunny. He always called Sue "Mrs. Snifkins" when they kept store.

"Oh, good morning, Mr. Huntley," Sue replied. She always called her brother "Mr. Huntley," when they kept store. Perhaps this was because he used to pretend to hunt for things on the make-believe shelves.

"What can I do for you this morning, Mrs. Snifkins?" asked Bunny, rubbing his hands as he had seen Mr. Gordon, the real grocer, do.

"I want some prunes, some coffee, some eggs, some sugar, some salt, some butter, some——" ordered Sue all in one breath.

"Stop! Stop! Wait a minute!" cried Bunny. "I can't remember all that! Now what did you say first?"

"Prunes," replied Sue.

There were some real prunes among the things the children were playing store with, and Bunny wrapped a few of these in a paper.

"Now some sugar," Sue ordered.

As real sugar was rather messy if it spilled on the floor, Bunny had some bird gravel, which was almost as good, and he pretended to weigh some of this out on an old castor that was the make-believe scales. Some real coffee beans were also wrapped up for Sue, and then for eggs Bunny used empty thread spools.

"Will that be all to-day, Mrs. Snifkins?" asked Grocer Huntley, when Sue had put the things in her basket.

"Yes, that's all," Sue answered, placing two large black buttons on the ironing board counter and getting back in change a small white button.

Sue went out with her "groceries," and soon came back for more. After her third trip, by which time she had bought nearly everything in the store, she said:

"Now I want to be storekeeper."

"All right," agreed Bunny.

Sue brought back the things she had pretended to buy, they were put on the shelves again, and Bunny became a purchaser while Sue waited on him.

Outside it still rained hard, as Bunny saw when he looked from the window. But it was fun in the house, keeping store. The children kept on taking turns, first one being the keeper of the store and then the other, until Bunny suddenly had a new idea.

"Oh, I know what we can do!" cried the little boy.

"What?" asked Sue.

"We'll play hardware store," Bunny said. "I'm tired of having a grocery. We'll keep hammers and nails and things like that."

"I think a grocery is more fun," said Sue.

"Nope! A hardware store is better," Bunny insisted. "I'll sell you washboilers, basins, tin pans and things like that, and knives and forks. We can have ever so many more of those things than we can have groceries."

"Well, maybe we can," Sue agreed, doubtfully.

"I'll make a high-up shelf, like those in the hardware store down town," went on Bunny. "I'll have things high up on the shelf, and I'll climb up on a ladder to get 'em, as they do down town."

"What you going to climb up on?" Sue asked.

"The stepladder."

"What you going to make a high shelf of?" Sue inquired.

"There's another ironing board down in the laundry," Bunny answered. "And I can get the washboiler and a lot of things. I'll put the other ironing board away up there, across the top of the two doors."

"That'll be awful high," said Sue, looking to where Bunny pointed. The pantry door and the one leading from the kitchen into the hall were close together on one side of the room. By opening these doors half way a board could be placed across their tops, making a high shelf. This was soon done, and on this shelf the big tin washboiler was placed, and also some tin pans from the pantry. Bunny climbed up on the stepladder to put the shelf and things in place.

Other articles for a hardware play-store were placed on the lower ironing board shelf, and then Bunny was ready for "Mrs. Snifkins" to come again. Sue had her button money all ready, the store was in order, and new fun was about to begin, when Mary, coming suddenly in from the hall and not knowing what the children were doing, pushed wider open the hall door.

Instantly there was a grand crash! Down came the upper shelf from the tops of the doors. Down came the washboiler and a lot of tin pans. My, what a racket there was!

And, worst of all, Bunny Brown himself was hidden from sight in that mess of ironing board, washboiler, and other things!

"Oh! Oh! Oh!" cried Sister Sue, dropping her basket and her button money, which rolled all over the floor. "Oh, dear!"

"Bless and save us!" cried Mary, the cook. "What has happened?"

Bunny Brown said nothing.

CHAPTER II

FEEDING THE ALLIGATORS

Mrs. Brown came hurrying into the kitchen from the living room.

"What has happened?" she asked. "What was that crash?"

It needed only one look to show her what had happened and what had caused the rattling, banging, crashing sound. On the floor, over and around the two chairs and the large ironing board, were the smaller board, the stepladder, the washboiler, two hammers, a lot of nails, many bread, cake, and pie pans, and some knives and forks.

"Where's Bunny?" asked Mrs. Brown.

Well might she ask that, for Sue's brother was not in sight, nor had he uttered a word since the accident.

"He—he's under there I—I guess," faltered Sue. She was not quite sure where Bunny had gone when that terrible crash came.

"Yes, I see his legs! I'll pull him out, Ma'am," offered Mary. "Oh, I hope nothing has happened to him!"

Mrs. Brown hurried to assist Mary in digging Bunny from under the wreckage of his hardware store. And while they are doing that I will beg a moment's time from those of you who have never before read any of these books, to tell you something of the two children who are to have some queer adventures in this present volume.

Bunny Brown and his sister Sue are well known to many of you children. Bunny and his sister lived with their father and mother, Mr. and Mrs. Walter Brown, in the town of Bellemere, on Sandport Bay, near the ocean. Mr. Brown kept a boat and fish dock, and one of his helpers was Bunker Blue, a young man who was very fond of Bunny and Sue.

In the Brown home were also Uncle Tad, who was Mr. Brown's relative, and Mary, the good-natured cook. There was also Splash, a big dog. And I might mention Toby, a Shetland pony. There were other pets to whom I will introduce you from time to time. Toby had been away from the Brown children for a while, but was now back again.

In the village were many friends of Bunny and Sue. Mrs. Redden, who kept a candy store, was a very special sort of friend, and she gave the biggest penny's worth of sweets for miles around. Mr. Gordon, as I have told you, kept a real grocery store, and then there was Mr. Jed Winkler, an old sailor who owned a parrot and a monkey named Wango. Mr. Winkler's sister, Miss Euphemia, did not like either Polly or Wango.

Charlie Star, George Watson, Mary Watson, Sadie West, Helen Newton, Harry Bentley, and fat Bobbie Boomer were all friends of the Brown children.

Now that you know the names of most of the characters who are to appear in this book, I might mention some of the other volumes. The first one was called "Bunny Brown and His Sister Sue," and told of their adventures around home. Then they went to Grandpa's farm, they played circus, they visited Aunt Lu in her city home, they went to "Camp Rest-a-While," and then they went to the Big Woods. After that they had exciting adventures on an auto tour, and you can imagine what joy was theirs when they were given a Shetland pony, that was named Toby.

Bunny Brown and his sister were always thinking up new ideas, and when they wanted to give a show few doubted but what they would succeed. They did, and made a goodly sum for a home for the blind. One of the trips the Browns made was to Christmas Tree Cove, and in the book of that name you will find their adventures set forth. They also made a winter trip to the South, and they had not long been back from that when the things happened that I have just told you about—the grand crash in the make-believe hardware store.

With the help of Mary and Mrs. Brown, Bunny was pulled from beneath the wreckage. At first the little boy could hardly speak, and his mother, no less than Mary and Sue, was beginning to get frightened. But suddenly with a gasp Bunny found his voice, and his first question was:

"Did you get hurt, Sue?"

"No," she answered. "But I guess you did."

"Only a little crack on the head," Bunny replied, rubbing the place that hurt. "But who knocked down my high shelf? Did Splash get in and wag his tail?"

Sometimes the big dog did this with funny results.

"I guess I knocked down your shelf, Bunny," said Mary. "I'm sorry, but I didn't know you had a board on top of the doors."

"Did you have that, Bunny?" asked his mother.

"Yes'm, I—I guess I did," Bunny had to admit. "It was a high shelf for our hardware store. I had the washboiler up there!"

"No wonder there was a crash!" exclaimed Mrs. Brown. "It's a wonder you weren't hurt!"

"I guess the big ironing board fell on the stepladder first, and stayed there, and the rest of the things didn't hit Bunny because he was under the board," explained Mary.

And that is about how it happened. Bunny was under a sort of arch formed by the stepladder and the two ironing boards, and so was saved from being hit on the head by the heavy things. One of the overturned chairs, however, had struck him in the stomach, and this had rather knocked his breath out, which made him unable to talk for a little while.

"Well, I'm glad it was no worse than this," said Mrs. Brown. "Mercy sakes, though, the kitchen is a sight!"

"I don't mind! I'll clean it up," offered good-natured Mary. "The children have to play something in the house when it rains out of doors."

"Yes," agreed Mrs. Brown. "But they could have kept on playing grocery store. They didn't need to make a high shelf and put the big washboiler up on it to fall down when the door was moved the least bit!"

"I did that," confessed Bunny, anxious that Sue should not be blamed for what was not her fault. "I didn't know anybody would push the door."

"Well, it's a mercy it was no worse," remarked his mother. "And now, after you have helped Mary pick up the things, go on with your playing. Can't you play grocery instead of hardware store, Bunny, my dear?"

"Oh, hardware store is nicer, and we have all the things now," Bunny replied. "But I won't make any more high shelves."

The washboiler, the pans, and the scattered knives and forks were picked up, and then Bunny and Sue went on playing, using only the low ironing board shelf, which was made over the seats of two chairs. They took turns keeping store and doing the buying, and had a great deal of fun.

But even making believe keep a hardware store gets tiresome after a while, especially if there are only two playing, and after a while Bunny Brown and his sister Sue wanted something else to interest them.

"'Tisn't raining quite so hard now," Sue observed, after a look from the window.

"That's right!" cried Bunny. "Oh, say! Maybe we can go out in the barn and feed our alligators!"

"That'll be fun," agreed Sue. "And I guess they're hungry; don't you, Bunny?"

"Yes, I guess so. Let's go ask mother if we can feed 'em."

"I know she'll say yes, so I'll get some scraps of meat from Mary," said Sue.

As the rain was slackening and as Mrs. Brown knew that the alligators might need food, she told the children they could go out to the barn if they put on their rubber boots and coats.

"Aren't you afraid the alligators will bite you?" asked Mary, as she cut up some bits of meat for the children.

"Course not; we aren't afraid!" boasted Bunny. "They're only little alligators, and they're real tame."

One of the long-tailed, scaly pets given to the children by Mr. Bunn had been brought from the South where the Browns spent part of the winter, and later Mr. Brown had gotten some others. The alligators were kept in a tank of water in the barn. Bunny and Sue wanted the alligators kept in the house, but Mrs. Brown insisted that the barn was the place for pets of that sort.

Out into the rain storm, which was now almost over, went Bunny Brown and his sister Sue to feed the alligators. There were three or four of the scaly creatures, and as the children drew near the tank the alligators came crawling out of the water up on some bits of wood and stone that made a resting place for them. For alligators cannot stay under water all the while, as can a fish. They must come out every now and then to get air.

"Oh, look at Judy!" cried Sue, dangling a piece of meat in front of the nose of one of the queer pets. "She's awful hungry!"

"And so is Jim!" said Bunny, feeding another of the creatures. They lifted up their long snouts, opened their mouths, and took in the pieces of meat.

"Where's Jumbo?" suddenly asked Sue. "I don't see him!"

"Maybe he got out!" said Bunny, for the largest of the pet alligators was not in sight. Not that Jumbo was very large, for though he was the biggest in the tank he was not more than ten inches long.

"Oh, here he comes!" cried Sue, as Jumbo swam up from the bottom of the tank. "I guess he was asleep."

"I guess so," agreed her brother. "Here, Jumbo!" he went on. "Here's some meat for you!"

"Jumbo's getting real big," said Sue, as she watched the largest of the pets.

"And Judy is growing," added Bunny. "I wish we had had these 'gators when we gave our show."

"Yes," agreed his sister. "Well, maybe we can have another show. Or we could put the alligators in a store the next time we play."

"Yes," said Bunny. "Only maybe you couldn't wrap up a 'gator in a piece of paper. He might bite his way out."

"That's so," said Sue. "Well, we could——"

But she did not finish what she was saying, for a loud barking suddenly sounded outside the barn. At this noise Bunny and Sue started on a run for the door.

CHAPTER III

SOMETHING IN A DESK

Splash, the dog, was barking loudly at something up in a tree near the barn. Bunny and Sue could not see what it was, but it was something that had caused Splash to get very much excited. He leaped up and down and ran in circles about the tree, barking loudly all the while.

"It's a cat!" exclaimed Sue.

"Can't be a cat," Bunny answered. "Splash likes all the cats around here."

"Maybe it's a strange cat," went on Sue.

"That's so," agreed Bunny Brown. "Here, Splash!" he called. "What you barking at a cat for?"

The only answer the dog made was to bark again.

Bunny and his sister, forgetting all about their pet alligators, ran to the foot of the tree, up in which was something that had caused Splash to cease his play in another part of the yard and run toward the barn. The rain had now stopped, and the sun was getting ready to shine.

"What is it, Splash? What is it?" asked Bunny, trying to peer up among the leaves of the tree.

"I see it!" suddenly cried Sue. "It's Wango, Mr. Winkler's pet monkey!"

"Oh, yes! I see it now!" called Bunny. "Here, Splash! Stop barking at Wango!" ordered the little boy. "Don't you know he's a friend of yours? Stop it, Splash!"

Splash finally ceased barking and sat down to look eagerly up into the tree. He would not have hurt the monkey, for the two animals were good friends. I suppose Splash had seen the monkey leaping from the branches of one tree into another, and, not realizing that it was his friend Wango, had given chase. Wango was a bit frightened at first, even by the barking of his dog friend Splash, and had taken refuge in the tree near the barn.

"Come on down, Wango! Come on down!" invited Bunny.

"Yes, please do," added Sue. "We won't let Splash hurt you. Don't you bark any more, Splash!" she cried, shaking her finger at the dog.

Splash whined. He really only meant to have a little fun with Wango. But the monkey did not come down. He clung to the tree branch with his hands and tail and looked at the children, whom he well knew, for they were kind to him.

"I know how to get him down," said Bunny. "You go into the house and get a piece of cake for him, Sue. Take Splash with you. Then Wango won't be afraid."

"All right," agreed the little girl. She was always ready to run errands like this when she and Bunny could have fun. "Come on, Splash!" she called, and the dog followed her, looking back once at Bunny, as if to ask why the boy, too, was not following. But Bunny stayed near the tree in which Wango still clung.

"Mother," cried Sue, tramping into the house in her rubber boots, "please may Bunny and I have some cake for Wango?"

"You can't go over to Mr. Winkler's in the rain," said Mrs. Brown. "You'd better stay out in the barn and feed your pet alligators."

"Oh, but the rain is over," Sue explained. "The sun is coming out. And Wango isn't over at his own home. He's up in one of our trees. Splash chased him up there, I guess, and barked at him. And he won't come down—I mean Wango won't. And will you please keep him in here till I take him out some cake. I mean," explained Sue, half out of breath, "you please keep Splash here in the house while I take some cake out to Bunny to feed Wango to get him down from the tree."

"My, what a lot of talk for a little girl!" laughed Mrs. Brown. "Well, I suppose Wango has run away again from Jed. You and Bunny may take the monkey back. Ask Mary to give you a bit of cake. I'll keep Splash in the house."

Sue got the cake, but it was rather difficult for Mrs. Brown to keep the dog in. He was eager to follow Sue back to the tree again. But it would be hard work to get Wango down, once the monkey was frightened, if Splash kept on barking, which he was pretty sure to do. He even barked loudly, Splash did, while he was being held in the house by Mrs. Brown.

Sue ran out with the cake to Bunny, who was waiting beneath the tree.

"Is Wango there yet?" the little girl wanted to know.

"Yes," Bunny answered. "But he's coming down a little."

And the monkey came down still farther when he saw the cake, of which he was very fond. He was soon perched on Bunny's shoulder, eating the treat, Sue feeding him little pieces one at a time.

"Let's take him back to Mr. Winkler's house," suggested Bunny, as the sun now came out bright and warm. "I guess the sailor will be looking for him."

"Yes, I guess so," agreed Sue.

Wango had a great habit of running away from his master's home, and, more than once, Bunny Brown and his sister Sue had taken back the sailor's pet. This they now did again, and as they knocked at the side door, Miss Winkler opened it.

"Here's your monkey back," said Bunny, after the first greetings.

"Huh! 'Tisn't my monkey!" declared Miss Winkler. "It's Jed's! I shouldn't ever worry if it never came home! Still, that isn't saying it's your fault, Bunny and Sue. I know you mean to be kind, and Jed will thank you, even if I don't. Wango, you rascal, why don't you stay away when you run off? I don't want you around! What with the poll parrot——"

"Polly wants a cracker! Polly wants a cracker!" shrieked the green bird.

"A fire cracker's what you ought to have!" sniffed Miss Winkler, who did not like the two pets her sailor brother had brought back with him from one of his voyages.

"Cracker! Cracker! Put the kettle on the fire! Polly wants a cracker!" yelled the bird, and Wango began to chatter, the two of them making such a racket that Miss Winkler held her hands over her ears while Bunny and Sue could not help laughing.

"Stop it! Stop it!" yelled the maiden lady, and finally the monkey and the parrot grew quiet.

"Put Wango in his cage, Sue, if you please," said Miss Winkler. "And I'll tell Jed, when he comes home, how good you were to bring Wango back—not that I want the creature, though. Well, it's cleared off, I'm glad to see. And now maybe you two will have a piece of cake for yourselves. I won't give Wango any, though!"

"Yes'm, I could eat a bit," said Bunny, with a smile.

"I like it, too," added Sue.

The children were soon having a lunch of cake and milk. Though Miss Winkler was a bit fussy over her brother's pets, yet she had a good heart, and she liked Bunny and Sue.

Through the little mud puddles, left after the rain, Bunny and Sue splashed their way back home. Their mother saw them coming, and, as Splash was making a great fuss at being kept in the house, she let the dog out. He ran to meet the children.

"What'll we do now?" asked Bunny, when they had told their mother about taking Wango home.

"Let's go down and wade in the brook," proposed Sue. "We have our boots on, and we won't have 'em on to-morrow. We'll have to go to school then, anyhow. So let's go wade in the brook now."

"All right!" agreed Bunny. "And we'll sail boats!"

With their dog, the children were soon splashing in the shallow brook, made a bit higher on account of the rain. They found some boards and made a raft, on which they pushed themselves about the wider part of the brook.

Splash climbed on the raft with them, and the children pretended they were Robinson Crusoe on a voyage.

"Well, we had a lot of fun to-day," sighed Bunny in contentment, as he and Sue were going to bed that night. "Lots of fun!"

"Yes," agreed his sister. "And to-morrow we have to go to school."

"Oh, well," Bunny remarked, "maybe we'll have fun there." The children had been kept at home on account of the heavy rain.

"We won't have any fun like the hardware store shelf falling down on you," laughed Sue, as she remembered the queer accident.

"No, I don't want anything like that," said Bunny. "Once is enough."

Early the next morning the children were ready for school. But, almost at the last minute, Bunny could not find his large pencil box.

"Where did you have it last?" his mother asked him.

"Oh, I remember! I saw it in the barn!" exclaimed Sue.

"That's right—we were playing school there day before yesterday," said Bunny. "I'll get it!"

He ran to the barn, got the pencil box, thrust it into his bag with his books, and trotted along with Sue.

Having to hunt for his pencil box at almost the last moment nearly made Bunny and Sue late for school. But they slipped into their seats just as the last bell was ringing. After the morning exercises, Bunny placed his pencil box and the books he did not need to use right away in his desk and went to his reading class.

It was when Bunny was doing his turn at reading up near the front platform that Sadie West, who sat in the seat next to Bunny, gave a sudden little cry.

"What is the matter, Sadie?" asked Miss Bradley, the teacher.

"Oh! Oh, if you please, Teacher, there's something in Bunny Brown's desk making faces at me!" exclaimed Sadie.

"Something making faces at you? What do you mean, Sadie?" asked Miss Bradley in surprise. "What is it?"

"It—it's a—a mouse!" cried the little girl.

"A mouse?" repeated the teacher.

"Yes'm! A mouse in Bunny Brown's desk!" and Sadie screamed.

At this some of the other children screamed, and there was much noise and confusion in the schoolroom.

CHAPTER IV

THE CORNER STORE

"Quiet, children! Quiet!" ordered Miss Bradley. "This is school, not the playground at recess. Now, Sadie," she went on, as soon as there was a little quiet in the room, "tell me again, and be careful what you say. What did you see?"

"Please, teacher, I saw a mouse in Bunny Brown's desk, and he made a face at me. I mean the mouse made a face at me—not Bunny!" Sadie made haste to explain, for she saw Bunny look at her when she made the statement about his desk and the mouse.

Sadie had left her seat beside Bunny's desk, and was now up front.

"How many other girls saw the mouse in Bunny's desk?" asked Miss Bradley.

No one answered.

"Raise your hands if you are afraid to speak," said the teacher, with a smile. She was beginning to believe that Sadie had imagined it all, or else that an edge of a book had looked like a mouse.

None of the girls raised her hands except Sadie West.

"Did any boy see the mouse?" Miss Bradley next asked.

"No, but I wish I had!" exclaimed Charlie Star. "If I'd see it I'd grab it!"

The other pupils giggled on hearing this.

"Quiet, children! Quiet!" begged the teacher again.

"Are you sure, Sadie, that you saw a mouse in Bunny Brown's desk?" asked Miss Bradley.

"Yes'm, I'm sure I did," was the answer.

"Bunny, did you bring a mouse to school?" Miss Bradley next asked. "I mean a pet mouse, for I know you and Sue have many pets. Did you bring a mouse to school, Bunny?"

"Oh, no, Teacher! I wouldn't do such a thing!" Bunny declared very earnestly.

"I didn't believe you would," said Miss Bradley, with a kind smile. "I think Sadie must be mistaken. But still, to quiet her—and all of you," she added, looking at the pupils, "I will look in Bunny's desk. I am quite sure I will find nothing more than a book or a piece of paper that may have moved, making Sadie think it was a mouse."

Miss Bradley went to Bunny's desk. All the desks in the room were of the sort with a lid that raised up and down on hinges, like the cover of a box. As Miss Bradley came near Bunny's desk she noticed that the top was raised a little way, leaving a crack of an opening. Bunny had put one of his books in hurriedly, and the desk lid rested on this.

As the teacher raised the desk lid and looked in, the room was very quiet. Some of the girls almost held their breaths. One of them covered her eyes with her hands, lest she might, by accident, see the mouse.

Sadie West leaned forward eagerly, anxious, in a way, that a mouse should be found, for that would make her story true, and she was sure, in her own mind, that she had seen a mouse. Bunny, too, looked eagerly at Miss Bradley, and so did Sue, from the other side of the room.

"Grab a book, everybody!" said Charlie Star in a hoarse whisper to the other boys. "Grab a book, and if the mouse runs out we'll bang him!"

Charlie was an active little chap, almost as lively as Bunny Brown himself.

Miss Bradley heard what Charlie said and, with the desk lid half raised, she said:

"No, boys! No throwing of books, if you please! Should there be a mouse in the desk I can call the janitor to get it out."

"Oh, let me get it out!" begged Bunny.

There was no time to say more, for now Miss Bradley had Bunny's desk lid fully raised. She looked inside for a moment, then with a queer look on her face she closed the desk again and moved away.

"Did you see it, Teacher? Did you see the little mouse—same as I did?" eagerly asked Sadie.

"No," answered Miss Bradley. "There isn't a mouse in the desk, but there is a little alligator!"

"Alligator!" cried the girls—that is, all but Sue.

"Alligator!" shouted the boys.

"Let's see it!" cried Charlie Star.

"Quiet, children! Quiet!" ordered Miss Bradley. Then, turning to Bunny she asked: "Did you bring that little alligator to school?"

"No'm," Bunny answered.

"Is it yours?" went on Miss Bradley.

"Well, I have some pet alligators home," Bunny admitted. "Half of 'em's Sue's. We got one of 'em down South, and Daddy bought the rest. But I didn't bring any to school. If you let me look I can tell if it's mine or Sue's."

"I'll help!" offered Charlie Star. "I know Bunny's alligators, too!"

"No, let Bunny manage his own pets," said the teacher. "Come here, Bunny, and see what really is in your desk. I can't understand how an alligator would get in there if you didn't bring it."

Bunny opened his desk cover, the other boys wishing they had his chance to "show off" this way right in the school room. Bunny looked inside and then laughed.

"Yes," he said, "it's Judy, the littlest alligator. She won't hurt anybody."

"But how did it get to school?" asked Miss Bradley.

"It's in my big pencil box," Bunny answered. "I brought my pencil box to school this morning, but I didn't open it and——"

"Teacher! Teacher! I know!" exclaimed Sue, raising her hand to show that she had something to tell.

"Well, how did it happen?" asked Miss Bradley.

"If you please, Teacher," said the little girl, "Bunny's pencil box was out in the barn where we keep the alligators. He left it there when we played school the other day. This morning Bunny couldn't find his pencil box, but it was out in the barn. He brought it in from there and we came to school."

"And I guess," said Bunny, finishing the story his sister had started, "that Judy climbed into my pencil box in the night and went to sleep there and I didn't see her."

This seemed to be as good an explanation as any, and was probably the way it had happened. Anyhow there was the little alligator in the pencil box inside Bunny's desk. The scaly creature had crawled in and then out, and when Bunny went up to recite the little creature had thrust its snout out beneath the partly raised lid. It was this that Sadie West had seen and thought was a mouse.

"Well, Bunny," said Miss Bradley, "I know it wasn't your fault, so we'll say nothing more about it. Only, after this, please look in your pencil boxes before you bring them to school."

"I will," promised Sue's brother.

"And now I'll excuse you from class while you take your alligator home," went on Miss Bradley.

"I can help him, Miss Bradley, if he wants me to," offered Charlie Star. "I know a lot about alligators."

"No, thank you," replied the teacher with a smile. "This alligator is so little I think Bunny can manage it alone. Now we will go on with our lessons!"

There was something like a sigh of disappointment among the children. For they had all welcomed the happening, since it gave them a sort of recess. But now they must pay attention to their books.

Bunny shut Judy up in his pencil box, as the easiest way of carrying the little alligator, and soon he was on his way home with his pet.

"Why, Bunny! what's the matter?" his mother asked, as he came into the house. "Why are you home?"

"I had to bring back one of the alligators," he explained.

"Ha! Ha!" laughed Uncle Tad. "Like Mary's lamb, the alligator followed you to school one day, did it, Bunny?"

"She didn't 'zactly follow me," Bunny explained, as he took his pet out to the tank in the barn. "I carried Judy in my pencil box, but I didn't know it."

Bunny went back to school and finished his lessons. And all the remainder of the day, when the pupils had a chance to speak, they talked of nothing but Sadie West, the "mouse" and Bunny's pet alligator. It was very exciting, all together.

When Bunny and Sue reached home that afternoon they found their mother on the steps waiting for them.

"I'll take your books," she told the children, "and I want you to go to the store for me. Mary started to bake a cake and found, at the last moment, she was out of baking powder. I want you to go for a box. You needn't go all the way to the big store. Stop at the little one on the corner—Mrs. Golden's, you know. She sometimes has the kind I want. Go to the corner store and get the baking powder."

"All right!" exclaimed Bunny, and he and Sue hurried off. They knew where Mrs. Sarah Golden's little corner store was located—just a few blocks from their home, much nearer than the big store where Mrs. Brown generally traded. Bunny and Sue had been in Mrs. Golden's store before, but not often, as it was rather out of the way, and such a small place that Mrs. Brown was afraid things would not be as fresh as at the larger grocery. Besides groceries, Mrs. Golden also kept "notions"—that is, pins, thread, hooks and eyes, and things like that. She also had candy and a few toys for sale.

"Her store isn't much bigger than our play store was, is it?" asked Bunny of Sue, as they reached Mrs. Golden's.

"Not much," agreed Sue. "Didn't we have fun when we played store?"

"Lots!" agreed Bunny. "And didn't the boiler make a big racket when it fell down?"

He and Sue laughed at remembering this, but their laughs died away as they entered the little corner store and heard groans coming from behind one of the counters. Groans and sighs greeted the children as they opened the door. No one was in sight.

"Oh, Bunny!" exclaimed Sue, frightened, "what you s'pose has happened?"

CHAPTER V

A NEW PUPIL

Though Bunny Brown and his sister Sue had not often bought things in Mrs. Golden's store, they knew the woman who kept the place, and she knew them, for she often called them by name as they passed when she was out in front. But now Mrs. Golden was not in sight, though the groans that came from behind one of the counters seemed to tell that she was there.

"Oh, Bunny, I'm afraid!" whispered Sue, standing in the opened door with her brother. "Don't let's go in!"

"Why not?" Bunny asked.

"'Cause maybe burglars have been here and maybe they've hurt Mrs. Golden!"

"Well, if they have, then we've got to help her," decided Bunny. "But burglars don't come in the daytime. They come only at night time."

"That's so," agreed Sue, growing bolder.

And then the groans stopped and the voice of an old lady said:

"Who is there, my dears? Some children, I know by your voices, but I can't see you. Don't be afraid, but come and help me."

"Where are you, and what's the matter?" asked Bunny.

"I'm down behind the notion counter," went on the voice. "I stepped up on a box to reach something from the shelf, and I slipped and fell. I'm not badly hurt, thank goodness, but I'm sort of wedged in here between the box and the wall, and I can't get up. If you can pull the box out I'll be all right."

"We'll do that!" cried Bunny, and he ran around behind the notion counter, on the side of the store where the needles, pins, and spools of thread were kept. Sue followed her brother.

There, just as Mrs. Golden had said, they found the old lady storekeeper. She was lying on the floor with a small packing box so wedged between her back and the side wall that she could not easily get up, especially as she was old and feeble.

"Oh, it's Bunny Brown and his sister Sue!" exclaimed Mrs. Golden, when she saw the children. "I'm so glad you came in! I was hoping some one would come in to help me. The breath was sort of knocked out of me when I fell, and I could only grunt and groan for a few minutes."

"We heard you," said Bunny.

"And I thought it was burglars," added Sue.

"Bless your hearts!" exclaimed Mrs. Golden. "Burglars wouldn't come to my poor, little store. Now just pull the box out and I'll be all right."

Bunny and Sue tugged at the box on which Mrs. Golden had been standing when she slipped and fell. It was hard work, but they managed to pull it out, and then Mrs. Golden, with a few more grunts and groans, could get up.

"Oh, my poor back!" she exclaimed, as she sank into a chair outside the counter.

"Is it broken?" asked Sue anxiously.

"No, not quite," was the answer, with a little smile. "But it's strained, and I expect I'll be lame for a while. Philip always told me not to stand up on things to reach the top shelves, and I guess he was right."

"Who is Philip?" asked Bunny.

"Philip is my son," was the answer. "He's a grown man, and he has to go off to work every day, though he helps me in the store as much as he can. I wouldn't want him to know I fell. It would only worry him, and he might make me give up my store. And I don't want to do that. I'm feeling better now. I'll be all right in a little while. Did you want something, my dears?" she asked, for she must not forget that she was a storekeeper.

"We wanted some baking powder," said Sue. "But we aren't in any hurry."

"We are in a little hurry," said Bunny. "'Cause Mary's got a cake partly made, but maybe——"

"Oh, I have baking powder," said Mrs. Golden quickly. "And I'll be glad to sell it to you. If I sold more things I'd make more money. Let me see now; I'm feeling sort of queer in my head on account of my tumble, but baking powder—oh, it's on one of the high shelves. I—I'm almost afraid to reach up for it."

"Oh, let me get it!" eagerly begged Bunny. "I like to climb up. I'd like to get it! I like to keep store!"

"So do I!" added Sue. "We played store the other day, and a lot of things fell down when Mary closed the door. We had a high shelf, too."

"Yes, one needs high shelves in a store," said Mrs. Golden. "But, Bunny, do you think you can reach up and get the baking powder?" she asked. "I can point it out to you."

"Sure, I can get it!" declared the little boy. "I'd love to."

"We don't want you to fall again," said Sue.

"That's very kind of you," replied Mrs. Golden. "Well, the baking powder is on the other side of my store—the grocery side. There it is," and with a bent and trembling finger she pointed out the tin boxes.

"Oh, that's an easy climb!" exclaimed Bunny, and he soon proved that it was by clambering up and getting the box of baking powder he wanted. Then he paid for it.

The children asked Mrs. Golden if they could help her further. She said she was feeling better and would soon be all right.

"But don't climb up any more," warned Sue.

"That's right," echoed Bunny. "Maybe we could help you tend store, Mrs. Golden. I'm a good climber."

"Yes, Bunny, I notice you are," said the old lady, with a smile. "And it is very kind of you, but you see I never could tell when some one might come in and want something from a high shelf. Unless you stayed here all the while it wouldn't be of much use."

"No, that's so," the little boy admitted. "I'd like to stay here all the while, though. I like to keep store!"

"So do I," added Sue.

"But children must go to school," said Mrs. Golden, with a smile. "I'll have to get my son Philip to put all the things on low shelves, I guess. Then I can reach them without climbing up. Run along now, Bunny and Sue. Your mother will be waiting for that baking powder."

Bunny and Sue told their mother what had happened at the store.

"Poor old lady!" sighed Mrs. Brown. "She is very poor, I'm afraid. We must buy more of our things there, Mary. It will be a help to her."

"Yes'm, it will," agreed the cook. "I often stop there when I want something in a hurry. She and her son are honest and hard-working."

"And I worked, too!" said Bunny. "I helped her tend store. I climbed up and got the baking powder."

"That was kind of you. But you, too, must be careful, son," his mother told him.

On their way to school the next day Bunny and Sue went past Mrs. Golden's store to ask how she was. They found her smiling and cheerful, little the worse for her tumble.

"My son Philip is going to make me some lower shelves," she said.

"Then I can help reach things down for you," exclaimed Sue, with a smile.

"Yes, dearie," murmured Mrs. Golden.

"Wouldn't it be fun if we had a little store like that?" said Sue to Bunny, as they hurried along, to school. "I mean a real store, with real things to sell, and we could take in real money."

"Yes, it would be lots of fun!" agreed Bunny. "But I don't s'pose it will ever happen."

However, something very like that was to happen, almost before the children knew it.

"Yes," went on Bunny, when they had almost reached the school, "it would be dandy to have a store like Mrs. Golden's!"

"Maybe you will have some day—when you grow up," replied Sue.

"That's a long way off," sighed Bunny, as he looked down at his little, short legs.

There was nothing to disturb the school classes that morning. No pet alligators were found in the desk of Bunny or any of the other pupils, and neither Sadie West nor any of the other girls thought she saw a mouse.

However, something happened in the afternoon. It was a warm day, early in summer, though the long vacation had not yet come. The windows were open and the bright sun streamed in.

After a period of study Miss Bradley called the first class in spelling. Bunny and Sue were in this division, and they went up to the front seats where Miss Bradley heard all recitations.

"Sadie West, please spell church," called Miss Bradley. Sadie spelled the word right.

"Sue Brown, please spell horse," called the teacher, and Sue did not make a miss.

"Now, Bunny, it is your turn," said the teacher, with a smile. "Your word is cracker."

Bunny paused a moment.

"C—r—a——" he began.

Then suddenly, sounding throughout the school room, a harsh voice cried:

"Cracker! Cracker! Give me a cracker!"

Miss Bradley hurriedly stood up beside her chair. What pupil had thus dared to speak aloud in school?

CHAPTER VI

A BUSY BUZZER

Bunny, Sue and the other children were just as much surprised as was Miss Bradley when that strange, harsh voice called out. And it needed but a look at the faces of her pupils to show the teacher that none of them had broken one of the rules of the classroom.

Bunny still held his mouth open, for he was half way through the spelling of the word "cracker." He was about to keep on, when once more the voice called:

"Cracker! Cracker! Polly wants a cracker!"

The sound came from the cloak closet on one side of the classroom.

"It's a parrot!" cried Charlie Star. "A poll parrot!"

"Yes, I believe it is," said Miss Bradley.

"You didn't bring a parrot to school to-day, did you, Bunny?" she asked.

"Oh, no, Ma'am!" he exclaimed, so earnestly that of course Miss Bradley believed him.

"But I know whose parrot it is," said Sue, eagerly.

"Whose?" asked the teacher.

"Mr. Winkler's! He's got a parrot and a monkey. They're always getting loose. Maybe the monkey's in the cloakroom, too, only the monkey can't talk like Polly," went on Sue.

"Keep your seats, children!" said Miss Bradley. "I'll look in the cloakroom. There is no need to be excited. A parrot will hurt no one, nor a monkey, either. Keep your seats!"

As she opened the cloakroom door the harsh voice again sounded more loudly than before.

"Bow! Wow! Wow!" it barked. "Cracker! Cracker! Polly wants a cracker! Let's have a song! Ha! Ha! Ha!"

Then it began what I suppose the bird thought was singing.

The children laughed, and so did the teacher.

Out of the cloakroom flew the parrot, fluttering up on the teacher's desk. There it perched, preening its feathers with its big beak and thick, black tongue, now and then uttering harsh squawks and making remarks, some of which could not be understood.

"Is this the parrot you meant, Sue?" asked Miss Bradley.

"Yes'm, that's Mr. Winkler's," answered Sue. "I can take it back to him if you want me to. Polly knows me."

"And he knows me, too!" exclaimed Bunny.

"And me!" eagerly added Charlie Star. "Let me and Bunny take him home, please?" he begged.

"Is that the way to say it?" remarked the teacher, for the room was more quiet now. "What should you have said, Charlie?"

"Let Bunny and me," corrected Charlie.

"That's right. Always speak of yourself last. It is more polite. Well, I think you and Bunny may take the parrot back to Mr. Winkler," went on the teacher. "Certainly we don't want him in our class, though he seems a bright bird."

"You ought to see Wango, the monkey, climb!" cried fat Bobbie Boomer, and all the other children laughed. "He's great!"

"Well, I think a parrot is enough for one day," remarked Miss Bradley, with a smile. "Take Polly home, Bunny and Charlie."

"Just see, Teacher, he's tame and he knows me," Bunny said, stroking Polly's head, a caress the parrot seemed to like. Polly perched herself on Bunny's shoulder, and then he and Charlie went out, envied by the other pupils.

"Oh that bird! Out again!" cried Miss Winkler, when Polly was restored to her. "I declare, I'll make Jed get rid of her and Wango! They're more bother than they're worth!"

"I'll take 'em if you don't want 'em!" offered Charlie Star.

"So will I!" said Bunny.

But as Miss Winkler usually made this threat three or four times a week (or every time the monkey or parrot got loose), and as Mr. Winkler had never yet given them away, it did not seem likely that he would do so now. So Bunny and Charlie had small hopes of owning either pet.

The boys went back to school, passing, on their way, the store of Mrs. Golden.

"Let's go in," suggested Charlie. "I want to buy a top!"

"All right," agreed Bunny.

"Well, boys, what can I sell you to-day?" asked Mrs. Golden, coming out from the little back room where she generally sat when there were no customers to wait on.

"Got any tops?" asked Charlie.

"A few," Mrs. Golden answered, "but not many. I'm going to have a new lot in next week. Good day, Bunny," she went on. "Did your mother like that baking powder?"

"I guess so," Bunny answered. Then he and Charlie began looking at the tops. But the kind Charlie wanted was not in the case, and after looking at several Charlie decided not to buy any.

"Here's a tin automobile I'm selling cheap," said Mrs. Golden, taking a red toy out from another case. "It's the last one I have, and I'll sell it to you for what it cost me—twenty-five cents. The regular price would be fifty cents. See, I'll wind it up for you."

This she did, setting it down on the floor. With a whizz and a buzz the auto darted across the store, bringing up with a bang against the low part of the opposite counter.

"Say, that's a dandy!" exclaimed Charlie. "I'd like to own that!"

"So would I!" agreed Bunny. "Only I haven't twenty-five cents."

"I have!" Charlie said. "I was going to spend only ten cents for a top, but I guess I'll buy this buzzer auto for a quarter."

"It's in good order," said Mrs. Golden. "I'm not going to keep such expensive toys after this. I'm getting too old to run a toy store as well as groceries and notions. I'm giving up most of my toys. But this is a good auto, Charlie."

"Yes'm, I'll take it," said the little boy, and he bought the auto.

"You can't take it to school with you," said Bunny, as he and his chum left Mrs. Golden's store.

"Yes, I can," answered Charlie.

"If teacher sees it she'll take it away."

"Well, she won't see it. I can put it in my coat pocket." This Charlie did, after a struggle, for the pocket was rather small and the toy auto rather large.

"It sticks out and shows," Bunny said, after the toy had been crowded in.

"I'll stuff my handkerchief over it," Charlie decided, and this was done.

Then the two boys went on to school, arriving just as it was time for recess, so they did not have to go back to their lessons right away.

"And I didn't have to spell!" laughed Bunny. "Though I did know how to spell cracker."

"Come on!" called Charlie. "We'll have some fun with my new auto! I'll let it run around the yard."

This he did to the delight of the other boys. As for the girls, they gathered on the other side of the school yard for their own particular recess fun.

Sue, Mary Watson, Sadie West, Helen Newton and some others raced about, playing tag and jumping rope.

"Oh, I know what we can do!" suddenly cried Helen, when they were all tired from having romped about playing tag.

"What?" asked Sue.

"Let's go down to the end of the yard where the men are digging, and see how big the hole is," suggested Helen.

"Oh, teacher said we mustn't!" exclaimed Sadie.

"Well, we won't go very close," went on Helen. "She just told us to be careful not to fall in. But if we don't go too close we can't fall in."

This seemed a safe way of looking at it, and the girls were curious to see what the workmen had done at the far end of the school yard. The laborers had been digging for some days, fixing water pipes, and had made a deep trench, so deep that when a man stood down in it only his head showed above.

Just now none of the men was near the hole, all having gone away to get other tools, and as the boys were busy playing at the other end of the yard, or watching Charlie's auto, the girls could explore the digging by themselves.

"It's nothing but a hole!" said Sue, in some disappointment, as they approached as near as they dared and looked in.

"I'd like to go down in it!" exclaimed Helen, who was rather daring.

"Oh!" cried Sue. "Come back! Don't go too close!"

But Helen did not heed. She went up to the very edge of the long, deep trench, and was looking in when suddenly her feet slipped out from under her, and down she went, sliding right into the hole!

"Oh! Oh!" she cried.

"Oh! Oh!" screamed the other girls, and in such excited voices that Miss Bradley came running out of the classroom and the boys crowded down to the end of the yard.

"What has happened?" asked the teacher.

"Helen Newton fell into the big hole!" cried Sadie West.

"Did the dirt cave in on her?" asked Miss Bradley.

Fortunately, it had not. The walls of the trench were firm and solid, and the only thing that had happened was that Helen was down in the deep trench, and could not get up by herself. She was crying now.

"Don't cry," said Miss Bradley. "You're all right. We'll soon get you out. Now you other boys and girls keep back from the edges, or you'll cause the sides to cave in and they'll cover Helen! Keep back, Bunny, Sue, every one!"

This was good advice, and as the other children moved back away from the trench there was less danger. Miss Bradley was just going to send one of the boys to call the janitor when two workmen came back. They broke into a run as they saw the crowd about their digging place, for they had told the teacher to keep the children away from it.

"There's been an accident!" said one man.

But it was not so bad as he feared, and he and his companion soon lifted Helen out on solid ground again, a rather frightened little girl, but not in the least hurt.

"I told you to stay away from that hole!" said Miss Bradley, rather severely. "I was afraid something like this might happen. It is fortunate it was no worse. Who started it?"

There was a moment's pause, and then Helen raised her hand. She had been crying.

"If—if you please, Teacher, I went there first," she stammered.

"Well, I think your fright has been punishment enough for you," said Miss Bradley kindly, "and we will say nothing more about it. But if any of you go near that hole again he or she will be kept in after school. It isn't that I mind your seeing what the workmen are doing, it is just that it would be dangerous for even grown folks to go too near the edge of the trench, and much more so for you little folk. So keep away from the hole. I hope the pipes will be in this week, and the hole closed up. Now do you all promise to keep away?" she asked. "Raise your hands!"

Every hand went up, for the boys and girls were fond of their teacher and did not want to cause her worry.

It was a solemn moment, for they all felt that something dreadful might have happened to Helen had the dirt caved in on her.

"Hands down," said Miss Bradley, and down they went.

Just then the bell rang. Recess was over, and the lines of boys and girls marched into the schoolhouse once again.

Charlie Star reached for his handkerchief, which he had again stuffed over his toy automobile after he had crowded that toy into his pocket when going back into school after recess. As he pulled out his handkerchief the auto came with it and fell to the floor.

Suddenly there was a strange buzzing sound in the room. Neither the teacher nor the girls knew what it was, but Bunny and the boys knew it was Charlie Star's new toy automobile which he had bought from Mrs. Golden.

With a buzz the busy auto ran from Charlie's desk straight down the aisle toward Miss Bradley, who was standing in front of her platform.

CHAPTER VII

THE BARN STORE

For a second or two Miss Bradley seemed to pay no attention to the buzzing sound which Bunny, Charlie, and some of the other pupils heard only too plainly. The teacher was busy thinking whether she had done enough talking to make sure her boys and girls would not again go near the deep hole in the school yard.

"I wouldn't want any of them to get hurt," thought Miss Bradley. "I had better scare them a little now than have any of them harmed the least bit."

She was thinking what else she might say, to impress on the pupils the danger of the hole, when she seemed to hear, for the first time, the buzzing of Charlie's auto.

"What's that?" asked Miss Bradley.

No one answered, except that, here and there in the room, a boy or girl snickered.

There was one queer thing about Charlie's new toy auto. It made a great deal of buzzing as the wheels whirred around when the wound-up spring made them do this, but the machine itself did not go very fast. It seemed to make a great fuss about getting anywhere, but it took its own time in doing it.

This was the reason why the auto, though it had been pulled out of Charlie's pocket with his handkerchief and had fallen into the aisle down which it ran, did not very soon get where Miss Bradley could see it. She could hear the buzzing sound, but she did not know what it was.

"Who is making that noise?" she asked again.

No one answered, for, truth to tell, neither a boy nor a girl in the room was causing the noise; though of course Charlie was to blame, in a way.

Miss Bradley was looking over the room, into the faces of her pupils. The buzzing sound kept up. It seemed to be coming nearer and nearer. The windows were open, and she thought a bee or a wasp might have flown in. But it would be a very large wasp or bee, indeed, which would make so loud a buzzing sound as this.

"Children——" began Miss Bradley, and then she suddenly stopped, for something struck her on the foot. And it was right near her foot that the buzzing noise sounded. But as she had walked a little way down from her platform, and her foot was partly under the first desk—that of fat Bobbie Boomer—Miss Bradley could not see what had struck her.

"Oh!" she cried, as she jumped back, rather startled.

Charlie Star and Bunny Brown could not help laughing right out loud. They knew what had caused all this excitement.

A moment later Miss Bradley knew also. For Charlie's buzzing auto, having struck her foot, turned aside and rolled out on the floor in front of her teaching platform, in plain sight. There the little red toy came to a stop, for its spring was fully unwound.

Charlie and Bunny stopped their laughing suddenly as the teacher looked down at them.

"Whose is this?" askcd Miss Bradley, in a voice she hardly ever used in the classroom, for her pupils were generally very orderly. "Who owns this automobile?" she asked, sternly.

Timidly Charlie Star raised his hand.

"If you please, Teacher, it's mine," he said. And such a weak little voice as it was! Not at all like the loud, hearty tones Charlie used when he called to Bunny, "first shot agates!"

Miss Bradley stooped over and picked up the toy. She placed it on her desk, and then, turning to face the children, she said:

"I am very sorry about this. I thought, after what had happened to Helen, that you were going to settle down and study your lessons. Why did you bring this auto to school, Charlie? And why did you take it out?"

Charlie was silent a moment, and then he answered, saying:

"I—I didn't exactly take it out, Miss Bradley. It came out when I took out my handkerchief. I—I didn't mean to do it."

"Very well then, you didn't," the teacher agreed, with a little smile, for she knew Charlie was telling the truth. "But why did you bring the auto to school at all?"

Then Charlie told of having bought the toy that morning, on his way to school with Bunny Brown.

"I didn't have time to go home with it after I bought it," he said, "so I put it in my pocket. We played with it at recess, and I forgot and wound it up and stuck it in my pocket. I didn't mean to let it get out and run down the aisle."

Miss Bradley wanted to smile, but she knew it would not be just the thing to do. So she said:

"Well, Charlie, I will excuse you this time. But please don't bring any more toys into the schoolroom. And now, as we have lost much time from our lessons, we must study extra hard to make it up. Come to me after school, Charlie, and I'll give you back your auto."

Miss Bradley put the toy in her desk for safe keeping, and went on with the lessons. But it was rather hard for the pupils to get their minds back on their studies, because so much had happened that day from the time the parrot had screeched "Cracker! Cracker!" in the cloakroom until Charlie's auto fell out of his pocket and went buzzing down the aisle to bang into the teacher's foot.

However, the day came to an end at last, and then, talking and laughing, the boys and girls ran out of doors. Charlie stayed after the others, and walked shyly up to the desk at which Miss Bradley sat, looking over some examination papers. The room was very still and quiet after the noise and excitement of the children's outgoing.

"Yes, Charlie. What is it?" asked Miss Bradley, as she saw him standing near her desk.

"If you please—my auto——"

"Oh, yes," and she opened her desk and handed it to him. "It is a cute little toy," and she smiled at Charlie.

"You ought to see it go!" he exclaimed eagerly, for Miss Bradley was really a friend to her pupils, and she knew how to make kites and spin tops almost as good as a boy.

"Here! I'll show you!" Charlie went on. "It's a dandy!"

Quickly he wound up the auto and set it down on the floor. The wheels buzzed and the little red car spun across the schoolroom floor.

Bunny Brown and George Watson, waiting outside for Charlie, wondered what was keeping their chum. They knew he had stayed in to get his plaything.

"Maybe she's going to make him stay in half an hour," suggested George.

"She didn't say she was," replied Bunny. "But maybe she's giving him a—a leshure." What Bunny meant was lecture.

"Let's look in," suggested George.

On tiptoes they went to a window whence they could see into the room. There they saw Miss Bradley winding up Charlie's auto, and they heard Charlie saying:

"You try it now, Miss Bradley! See how nice it runs!"

And as the surprised watchers looked on, their teacher started the toy across the floor as Charlie had done. For, following the first showing of his plaything, Charlie had offered to let his teacher wind it, and she had agreed.

"Yes, it is a cute toy," said the teacher, as the auto banged into a side wall and stopped. "But we mustn't play with it in school hours."

"Oh, no'm!" agreed Charlie, and then he hurried outside, where Bunny and George were waiting for him.

"Say, you ought to see!" exclaimed Charlie, half breathless. "She ran the auto herself!"

"We saw her," said Bunny.

"She's a dandy teacher all right!" declared George.

One Saturday morning Bunny and Sue came downstairs to breakfast at the same hour as on other days. Usually this did not happen, for on Saturdays they were allowed to remain in bed a little longer than on days when they had to go to school.

"Well, what does this mean?" asked Uncle Tad, who was finishing his meal and reading the paper at the same time. "This is Saturday, isn't it? Unless I have on the wrong glasses!" he added, as he looked at the calendar on the wall.

"Yes, it's Saturday," said Bunny.

"Then why are you up so early?" asked Uncle Tad.

"'Cause a lot of the boys and girls are coming over, and we're going to play store out in our barn," explained Sue. "You can come and buy something if you want to, Uncle Tad."

"Thanks! Maybe I will!" chuckled the old soldier. "Are you going to sell any inside outside cocoanuts flavored with saltmint?" he asked.

"What are those?" Bunny inquired.

"Oh, he's only joking!" declared Sue, as she saw a twinkle in the eyes of Uncle Tad. And of course he was joking.

"Well, maybe I'll look in and see what you do have to sell in your barn store," he said, as he left the table.

Bunny Brown and his sister Sue were not long in finishing their breakfast, and then they hurried out to the barn where they were to keep store. Bunny and Sue had found some boards and boxes out there which would make fine shelves for a pretend store.

"We'll put the shelves up before the others get here," said Bunny.

"Yes," she agreed. "But what kind of store are you going to play? Are you going to have washboilers and tin pans?"

"No, I guess not," said Bunny, after thinking about it a moment. "We'll keep a store like Mrs. Golden's."

"Yes, that will be nice," agreed Sue. "Here, Splash!" she cried. "Get out of there! That box isn't for you to sleep in!" For the big dog had crawled into one of the boxes that were to form the store shelves. Splash was curling up most comfortably.

"We'll use him for a delivery dog," said Bunny. "We'll tie a basket on his neck and he can take the groceries and things to different places."

"Oh, that will be fun!" laughed Sue, clapping her hands. "Here comes Helen!" she cried a moment later, and then, with joyous shouts and laughter, a number of children came running into the Brown yard, ready to play barn store.

CHAPTER VIII

IN A HOLE

"What things are you going to sell?"

"Who's going to tend store?"

"I want to be cashier!"

These were some of the things the boys and girls shouted as they ran into the barn where Bunny Brown and his sister Sue were waiting for them to play store. Charlie Star, Helen Newton, fat Bobbie Boomer, Harry Bentley, George and Mary Watson and Sadie West were among the boys and girls who came crowding into the barn, for the day before Bunny and his sister had invited them to spend Saturday in having fun.

"We'll take turns tending store," explained Bunny, after he had shown his playmates the shelves and boxes that were to be used for shelves.

"And we're going to have our dog Splash deliver things with a basket on his neck," explained Sue.

"I should think it would be more fun to hitch up your pony Toby to the basket cart and have him to deliver things," remarked Helen.

"We thought of that," replied Bunny. "But Bunker Blue has taken Toby down to the boat dock. He has to do some errands for my father, so we can't have Toby."

As Bunny and his sister had played this game more than the others, they were allowed to lay out the plans. Bunny showed the boys how the boards were to be put across the boxes to make shelves, and Sue took the girls down to the brook to gather little pebbles and the shells of fresh water mussels which were to be used for money, as there were going to be so many "customers" for the barn store that Mrs. Brown's buttons would not be enough to make change.

"What things are we going to sell?" asked Charlie, as he began pulling something from his pocket.

"Oh, we'll get stones, sand, gravel, some leaves, pieces of bark, twigs, and things like that," Bunny explained. "But what you got in your pocket, Charlie?"

"My wind-up auto. I thought maybe we could use it in the store."

"How?"

"Well, it could be like a cash register. You see," Charlie went on, "somebody's got to be the cashier just as in a big store. We'll have different clerks, and when anybody buys anything they must pay the money to whoever is clerk."

"Yes," agreed Bunny, who understood thus far.

"Then," went on Charlie, "the clerk must put the money the customer pays into my auto, and send it on a plank up to the cashier's desk. The cashier will make change and send it back in the auto."

"Oh, that'll be great!" cried Bunny. "And I guess you ought to be the cashier for thinking it up, Charlie."

"Well, maybe I ought, 'cause it's my auto," Charlie said. He had been hoping for this all along. "Now I'll make myself a place to be cashier," he went on, "and I'll fix up a long plank for the auto to run back and forth on. One winding will bring it up to me and back to the clerk."

When the other children heard this plan they were much delighted. Soon the store was ready for business. Boards had been placed across the boxes and a tier of shelves made, the top one so high that a long box had to be used like a stepladder to reach it. On the shelves were placed different things picked up around the barn, in the yard, and in the patch of woods not far away, or brought from the shore of the brook.

Then the boys and girls divided themselves up, some were to be customers to buy things in the store, while others were to be clerks to wait on the customers. Charlie took his place at the end of the tier of shelves to act as cashier. From the end of the shelves to his box ran a long narrow plank on which the auto change-carrier was to run.

Finally everything was ready, even to torn pieces of newspaper in which the things bought were to be wrapped. Splash was on hand with a basket tied to his neck to deliver the goods. And each customer had picked out a certain part of the barn as his or her "home" where the things were to be delivered.

"All ready!" called Bunny Brown. He and Sue were to be clerks in the store at first; afterward they would take a turn at being customers.

"I want a pound of sugar!" ordered Sadie West, coming up to Bunny, standing behind his part of the front counter.

"Yes, Ma'am. A pound of sugar!" repeated Bunny, scooping up some sand in a clam shell. "Nice day, isn't it—Mrs. er—Mrs.——"

"Snyder is my name," said Sadie. "I'm Mrs. Snyder and I live at Oatbin Avenue," she added, as she looked toward the part of the barn she had picked out for her "house." It was near Toby's oat bin.

"Yes, Ma'am," answered Bunny. "I'll send it right over to Oatbin Avenue."

He wrapped up the sand-sugar in a piece of paper and took the black mussel shell which Sadie handed him as her "five-dollar bill." Bunny placed the shell in the automobile, and started it up the plank to where Charlie waited. Taking out the large shell, Charlie put in two smaller ones and a white stone. This was "change."

Back whizzed the auto down the plank until it reached Bunny, who took out the "change" and handed it to "Mrs. Snyder."

"Please send my sugar right over," she ordered.

"Yes, Ma'am, it will go on the first delivery," Bunny answered, as he had heard Mr. Gordon, the real grocer, often say.

"Here, Splash!" called Bunny, and his dog, with the basket on his neck, came running up, wagging his tail.

"Oh, look out!" cried Sue, who was acting as a clerk next to Bunny.

"What's the matter?" Bunny asked.

"Splash is wagging his tail so hard that he'll knock down my eggs!" complained Sue.

Of course the "eggs" were only pine cones from the woods near by, but when you are playing store you must pretend everything is real, or else it isn't any fun.

"Keep your tail still, Splash!" cried Bunny. But the dog seemed only to wag it the harder.

Splash might have knocked down all the "eggs" and done other damage in the store had not Bunny placed Mrs. Snyder's sugar in the basket and sent his pet to deliver the make-believe sweet stuff.

And Splash delivered it very carefully, too. Sadie had gone back to her home at " Oatbin Avenue" to wait for her sugar, and when it came she took it from the basket on Splash's neck. Then the dog went back to the barn store to run on more delivery errands.

This was a sample of the way Bunny, Sue, and their friends played that Saturday morning. Now and then they would change about, some who had been clerks becoming customers and the customers clerks.

Of course accidents happened. Splash wagged his tail so hard that he knocked over a box of prunes, scattering them on the barn floor. Even if the prunes were only little black stones it wasn't just the thing for Splash to do, and Sue scolded him for it. But Splash didn't seem to mind.

Another time, when the dog had been sent to deliver some ice-cream (which was really some white sand from the brook) to Mrs. Leland Sayre, who lived at Straw Terrace (Mrs. Sayre being Mary Watson), an accident happened. Splash was on his way to Mrs. Sayre's home when he heard another dog barking outside the barn.

With a bark of greeting Splash dashed out, spilling the "ice-cream" all over the barn floor.

"Oh, dear! And I wanted it for a party!" said Mrs. Sayre.

But of course it was all in fun.

More than once the change auto ran off the plank, either on its way to the cashier or coming back, and spilled the money all over the barn floor. But that could not be helped.

"Only it isn't good for my auto," said Charlie.

"We'll put some straw down on the floor so when it falls it won't get bent," said Bunny, and this was done.

All morning the children played store in the barn, selling the things over and over again. Splash got tired of being a delivery dog after a while, and Bobbie Boomer said he'd take his place. Bobbie was more to be depended on than Splash, who, try as he did, would sometimes deliver things to the wrong houses.

When noon came the neighboring children were talking of going home to lunch, but Mrs. Brown gave them all a pleasant surprise, including Bunny and Sue, by asking all the boys and girls to remain and have something to eat, served in the barn.

"Oh, what fun!" cried Sadie West.

"The best ever!" declared Charlie Star. "I'm glad I came!"

Lunch over, the playing of store went on again, until first one and then another began to tire, and it was given up. Then they put away the planks and boxes and played tag and hide and seek until it was time for supper, when the boys and girls went home.

"We've had a lovely time!" they said to Bunny and Sue.

Just before supper Mrs. Brown needed something from the store.

"I'll go get it," offered Bunny. "I'll get it at Mrs. Golden's."

"I'll go with you," said Sue, and soon they were at the little corner grocery.

"How are you to-day, Mrs. Golden?" asked Bunny, as the old woman was getting the yeast cake he had been sent for.

"Oh, pretty well," she answered, with a cheery smile on her kind but wrinkled face. "I'd like it if I wasn't so stiff, but then we can't have all we want in this world."

"We played store in our barn to-day," said Sue, looking around at the various shelves filled with many articles.

"Did you, dearie? That was nice. I guess it's easier to play store than it is to keep one really," said Mrs. Golden.

"Oh, I'd like to keep store!" declared Bunny Brown. "Only, how do you remember where everything is?" he asked. "There's such a lot of stuff!"

"Yes, there is," agreed Mrs. Golden. "And sometimes I forget. But I'm getting old, I reckon. There's your yeast cake. Now run along, and be careful when you cross the street."

"Yes'm, we will!" promised Bunny, as he took Sue's hand.

"Maybe, when vacation comes, Mrs. Golden will let us help her in her store," said Bunny to his sister, as they neared their home.

"Oh, maybe!" Sue agreed. "And it soon will be vacation, won't it?"

"Yes," said Bunny. "I wonder where we'll go this summer."

"I wonder, too," mused Sue. "If we could stay at home and have a real store it would be fun!"

Bunny agreed to this.

Several days passed. The hole in the school yard was filled up so there was no further danger of any of the boys or girls falling in. Charlie did not again bring his toy auto to school.

But something else happened.

One afternoon Charlie Star walked home with Bunny and Sue from school. Bunny had made a new sailboat, and he wanted Charlie to see it make the first voyage down the brook which ran back of the Brown home.

"May I come, too?" asked Sue, as Bunny carried his little vessel down to the stream.

"Sure, let her come," advised Charlie.

"All right," called Bunny, and Sue ran along after the boys.

But Bunny and Charlie were so interested in sailing the new boat that they did not pay much attention to Sue after reaching the brook. They watched the wind puff out the sails and Charlie was just going to ask Bunny if he would trade the boat for the toy auto when there came a loud scream from Sue, who had wandered off by herself.

"Oh, Bunny! I've fallen in! I've fallen in!" cried Sue.

"Oh, she is in!" exclaimed Charlie, glancing upstream.

"And there's a deep hole there!" shouted Bunny, darting away. "Come on, Charlie! Help me pull Sue out of the hole!"

CHAPTER IX

UP A LADDER

Charlie Star needed no second urging. Bunny had forgotten all about his toy ship, but Charlie gave one look and saw that it had safely blown on shore. Then Charlie sped after his chum.

"We're coming, Sue! We're coming!" cried Bunny. "Don't be afraid!"

"We'll get you out!" added Charlie.

The brook that ran back of the Brown house was rather deep in places, and some of these places were near shore where the bank went steeply down into the water. It was at one of these places that Sue had fallen in.

The little girl had been looking for "sweet-flag." This is the root of a plant something like the cat-tail in looks—that is, it has the same kind of long, narrow ribbon-like leaves.

But while the root of the sweet-flag is pleasant to gnaw, though a trifle smarty, the root of the cat-tail is of no use—that is, as far as Sue could tell. She wanted some sweet-flag, but not cat-tail root, and to find out which was right she had to pull up many of the long, green streamers. If Sue had known how to tell the difference otherwise it would have been easier.

It was in bending over to pull up some of the flag roots that she had leaned too far, and suddenly she found herself in the water. She had slipped off the muddy bank at a place where it was steep and the water was deep.

Luckily Sue had slipped in feet first, and now she was standing in water over her waist, yelling for Bunny to come and help her.

Breathless, the two boys reached the little girl. They could see then, that she was in no special danger, since the water was not over her head. If Sue had fallen in head first instead of feet first that would have been sadly different.

"Come on out! Come on out!" cried Bunny, reaching his hand toward his sister.

"I—I can't!" she answered.

"Why not?" Charlie asked.

"'Cause I'm stuck. I'm stuck in the mud!" Sue answered.

"Oh!" exclaimed Bunny. "Then we have to pull you out!"

"That's right!" said Charlie Star. "I'll help!"

"Look out you don't fall in yourselves!" warned Sue, as they held out their hands to her. "It's awful slippery!"

And the bank was, as Charlie and Bunny soon found, for Charlie nearly slid in as Sue had done and Bunny almost followed. But by digging their heels in the slippery mud they held on and soon they had pulled Sue out of the hole.

But, oh, in what a sad plight was the little girl!

She was soaking wet to a line above her waist, and she was splashed with water above that, some mud spots being on her face, one on the end of her nose making her appear rather odd. Her shoes and stockings were covered with black, mucky mud.

"Oh! Oh, dear!" exclaimed Sue, looking down at her legs, and began to cry.

"Don't cry!" advised Charlie.

"I—I can't help it!" wailed Sue. "And there's something on my nose, too!"

"It's only a blob of mud," said Bunny. "I'll wipe it off," and he did, very kindly.

"Look—look at my shoo-shooes!" sobbed Sue.

"Splash 'em in the water," advised Charlie. "Sit down on the bank, Sue, and splash your feet in the water."

"What'll I do that for?" she asked, through her tears. "I'm wet enough now!"

"Yes, I know," said Charlie. "And you can't get any wetter by dabbling your feet and legs in the water. But it will wash off the mud. You might as well wash it off."

"That's right," agreed Bunny. "Your legs will dry better if they are just wet, instead of being wet and muddy, Sue. Dabble 'em in the brook."

Sue thought this must be good advice, since it came from both boys. She was about to sit down near the place where she had slid into the brook, but Charlie said:

"No, not there! That water's all muddy. Come on down to a clean place."

This Sue did, sitting on the grassy bank and thrusting her feet and legs into the water up to her knees, splashing them up and down until most of the mud was washed from her stockings and shoes.

"Now we'll take you home," said Charlie.

"No!" exclaimed Sue. "I don't want to go home!"

"You don't want to go home?" repeated Bunny. "Why not? You have to get dry things on, Sue! Mother won't scold you for falling into the brook when it wasn't your fault!"

"I know she won't," Sue said. "But—but—I'm not going in the house looking all soaking wet! There's company—some ladies came to call on mother before we went out to play—and they'll see me if I go in the front door. I'm not going to have them laugh at me!"

"We'll take you in the side door then," offered Bunny.

"That'll be just as bad," whimpered Sue. "They can see me from the window."

"Well, then we'll go in the back way," Charlie proposed.

"No!" sobbed Sue. "If I go in the back way Mary'll see me, and she'll say, 'bless an' save us!' and make such a fuss that mother'll come out and it will be as bad as the front or side door!" complained the little girl. "I don't want to go home all wet!"

"But you'll have to!" insisted Bunny. "You can't stay out here till you get dry. You must go to the house, Sue!"

"Not the front way nor the side way nor the back way!" Sue declared.

"Then how are you going to get in?" asked Bunny. "Do you want to go in through the cellar?"

"I'd have to come up in the kitchen," objected Sue, "and Mary would see me just the same and she'd say, 'bless an' save us!'"

"Well, but how are you going to get in?" Bunny demanded. "There isn't any other way."

"Yes, there is!" suddenly exclaimed Charlie.

"How?" asked Bunny Brown.

"Up the painter's ladder," went on Charlie. "They're painting the roof of your sun parlor. And the ladder's right there. We can get Sue up the ladder to the roof of the sun parlor, and there's a second-story window she can get in so nobody can see her, and change her things."

"Oh! A ladder!" gasped Sue, when she heard how Charlie and her brother planned to get her into the house unseen by company. "A ladder!"

"Sure!" cried Bunny. "That's the best way! Charlie and I'll help you up."

"You won't let me fall?" asked Sue.

"Course not!" declared Charlie. "I've climbed lots of ladders!"

"So have I!" boasted Bunny Brown. "And so have you, Sue Brown!"

"And can't anybody see me if I go up the painter's ladder?" asked Sue, who was feeling most uncomfortable, being clammy and wet.

"Nobody'll see you!" declared Charlie. "The ladder's away off on one side of the sun parlor. Mary can't see you from the kitchen, and your mother and the company can't see you."

"Is the painter there?" Sue went on. She was asking a good many questions and making a number of objections, I think.

"No, the painter isn't there," Charlie said. "I saw him going back to the shop after more paint when we came down here."

"All right then!" sighed Sue. "Help me up the ladder!"

Cautiously the children approached it. There the ladder stood, a big one, on a long slant leading from the ground to the roof of the one-story sun parlor. From the roof of this extension were several windows Sue could climb into, one opening from her own room.

No one was in sight, and the painter had not come back. Sue was just starting up the ladder, with Bunny going before her and Charlie following her, when the little girl happened to think of something else.

"S'posin' the roof's just been painted?" she asked. "How can I walk on it?"

This was a poser for a moment until Charlie exclaimed:

"If it is I'll get some boards and we can lay them down to walk on."

Sue had no further excuse for not going up the ladder, and she began to climb. She reached the top, and it was found that the painter had spread his red mixture on only part of the roof. There was room enough to walk on the unpainted part to her room window.

She was just climbing in, with the help of the boys, when she suddenly noticed something that made her exclaim:

"Oh, look! How did that happen?"

CHAPTER X

THE LEGACY

"What's the matter? What's happened?" asked Bunny Brown. "Are you going to fall, Sue?"

He was helping his sister on one side to climb in the window, and Charlie was on the other side of the little girl.

"No, I'm not going to fall," Sue answered. "But look at my dress! It's all red paint!"

And so it was! In addition to being wet and muddy her skirt was now covered with big blotches of red paint—the same kind of paint that was being put on the roof.

"How did it happen?" went on Sue, almost ready to cry again. "I didn't step in any paint, did I?"

"Even if you did I don't see how it got on your dress," said Charlie Star.

"There's some on me, too!" cried Bunny Brown. "There's some on my pants!"

"And I'm daubed just like you!" cried Charlie. "We're all three painted!"

And they were, only Sue had more of it on her dress than the boys had on their clothes.

"It must have been on the ladder," decided Charlie. "The painter man got some of his red stuff on the ladder and we got it on us."

"Oh, dear!" sighed Sue. "Now after my dress is dry and I brush the mud off mother will see the red paint. Course I'd tell her, anyhow, but I wish she wouldn't see it first!"

However, there seemed no help for it. All three of the children had red paint on their clothes, and paint, you know, can't be brushed off. When it's on it stays, unless turpentine, or something like that, is used to take it off.

Sue, and the boys, too, had hoped that Mrs. Brown would not know what had happened. It wasn't that they wanted to deceive, or fool, her, but Sue wanted to tell of the accident at the brook in her own way and time. She really did not want to cause her mother worry when Mrs. Brown had company. And Mrs. Brown would certainly begin to ask questions when she saw those red spots on Sue's dress.

"Oh, dear!" sighed Sue again, and she seemed about to burst into tears. Neither Bunny nor Charlie knew what to do.

"Oh, dear!" sighed Sue for the third time.

Suddenly the three children saw the upper end of the ladder—the part that was raised up over the roof of the sun parlor. They saw this part of the ladder moving.

"Oh, somebody's coming up!" exclaimed Charlie.

"Maybe it's mother!" wailed Sue. "Oh, help me get in the window! I don't want her to see me this way!"

"Mother wouldn't be coming up the ladder!" declared Bunny. "What would she be coming up the ladder for?"

"That's so!" agreed Charlie. "I guess she wouldn't."

"But somebody's coming up!" declared Sue, and this was very plain to be seen. The ladder shook more and more.

Wonderingly the children watched it, and then there came into sight, above the roof of the sun parlor, the head and shoulders of the painter. He looked surprised as he saw the children, and then a cheerful smile spread over his face as he said:

"Well, you've been getting daubed up, I see!"

"Ye-yes," faltered Bunny. "We got some of your paint on us!"

"'Tisn't my paint!" laughed the painter. "It's your father's, Bunny. I got this paint down at his boat dock to paint the roof of this sun parlor. I don't mind how much of it you daub on yourselves. 'Tisn't my paint, you know!"

"But we don't want it on us!" exclaimed Sue. "Oh, I fell in the brook and I got all muddy and now I'm all covered with paint! Oh, dear!"

Sue was almost crying again, and the painter who at first had thought the children were merely playing, now began to understand that something was wrong.

"What's the matter?" he asked.

Then the story was told, of why the boys had helped Sue climb up the ladder to get into her room so her mother and the company would not see her in her soiled dress.

"But now we're all paint!" wailed Sue.

"Well, never mind!" said the good-natured painter. "I can take those paint spots out for you, if that's all you're worrying about."

"Oh, can you?" eagerly cried Sue.

"How?" asked Charlie Star, who was a rather curious little chap.

"Will you?" asked Bunny Brown, which was more to the point.

"I can and will!" said the painter. "Wait until I get some clean rags and my turpentine."

He want back down the ladder, but soon came up again, with a can of something with a strong, but not unpleasant smell. Bunny remembered that smell. Once when he was little, and had a bad cold, his mother had rubbed lard and turpentine on his chest.

"This turpentine will take the paint out when it's fresh," said the painter. "Stand still now."

He wet the rag in some turpentine, which, as you know, is the juice, or sap, of the pine and other trees. It is used to mix with paint, which it will dissolve, or melt away after a fashion. It also helps the paint to dry more quickly when spread on a house or bridge.

With the turpentine rag the painter rubbed at the red spots on Sue's dress, and then, having taken those out, he began on Bunny and Charlie. But the boys wanted to take out their own paint spots, and the painter let them do it.

"There you are," he finally said. "I guess they won't show now."

"And my dress is nearly dry!" exclaimed Sue. "Oh, I'm so glad. Mother won't know until I tell her. And of course I'll tell her," she quickly added.

Sue was as good as her word. After she got into her room and the boys had climbed down the ladder to go back and play with Bunny's little ship, Sue changed into dry clothes.

Then, after the company had gone, she told her mother all that had happened.

"I suppose it couldn't be helped," said Mrs. Brown with a smile. "I mean about falling into the brook. But it would have been just as well to come and tell me at once, Sue, instead of climbing the ladder. You might have fallen."

"I didn't want the company to know about it, Mother!"

"That was thoughtful of you. But if you had fallen off the ladder the company would have known about that, and it would have been much worse than just being seen in a wet and muddy dress."

"Oh, I couldn't fall with Bunny and Charlie to help me!" declared Sue.

That evening, just before supper, after Charlie Star had gone home and Bunny and Sue were playing out in the side yard, Mary called to them, asking:

"Do you children want to run to the store for me?"

"Yes," answered Bunny, and Sue inquired:

"What do you want?"

"A little pepper," was the answer. "I forgot that we were out and didn't order any when the grocery boy called to-day."

"We'll get it at Mrs. Golden's corner store!" said Bunny. "She keeps pepper."

"All right," Mary agreed. "Wait and I'll get you the money. We don't charge things at her store."

A little later Bunny Brown and his sister Sue, hand in hand, entered Mrs. Golden's little store.

"Well, my dears, what is it to-day?" asked the old lady, with a smile.

"Some pepper, if you please," answered Sue.

"Red or black?" asked Mrs. Golden.

Bunny and Sue looked at one another. This was something they had not thought about. Which did Mary want—red or black?

Seeing that the children were puzzled, Mrs. Golden said:

"What is your mother going to use it for, my dears?"

"Mother didn't tell us to get it," replied Bunny. "It was Mary, our cook, who sent us after it, 'cause she forgot to get any for supper."

"Oh, then it's black pepper she wants, I suppose," said Mrs. Golden. "She wouldn't want red pepper unless she were putting up pickles or something like that. I'll give you black pepper."

She started to rise from her chair, for she had been seated near the back of the store, but seemed so old and feeble that Bunny and Sue felt very sorry for her. When ladies got as old as Mrs. Golden seemed to be they ought always to rest in easy chairs, Bunny thought, and not have to get up to wait on a store.

Mrs. Golden grunted and groaned a little as she pushed herself up from the arms of the big chair.

"Are you terrible old?" asked Sue.

"I'm pretty old, yes, my dear," said Mrs. Golden. "But I don't mind that. It's the stiffness and the rheumatism. It's hard for me to get about, and the black pepper's on a high shelf, too. If my son Philip was only here he'd reach it down for me."

"Where is Philip?" asked Sue.

"Oh, he's gone to the city on business. He hopes to get a little legacy."

"What's a leg-legacy?" asked Bunny. "Is it something to sell in the store?"

"Bless your heart, no!" laughed Mrs. Golden. "A legacy is money, or property, or something like that which is left to you. If some of your rich relations die they leave money in the bank, or a house and lot, and it comes to you. That's a legacy."

"Did some of your rich relations die?" asked Sue.

"Well, an old man, who wasn't a very close relation, died," said the storekeeper. "There was some talk that he might leave me something, and Philip went to the city to see about it.

"But, dear, me! things are so uncertain in this world that I don't believe I'll get anything. There's no use thinking about it. I don't want to be disappointed, but I would like to get some money!"

Poor old lady! She seemed very sad and feeble, and the children felt sorry for her.

"Let me see now," went on Mrs. Golden. "Was it salt you said you wanted, Bunny?"

"No'm, pepper—black pepper."

"Oh, yes, black pepper! And it's on a high shelf, too. I wish Philip was back. He'd reach it down for me. I don't believe he'll get that legacy after all. Let me see now—pepper—black pepper——"

"Let me get it!" begged Bunny. "I can climb up on a high shelf!"

"So can I!" cried Sue. "I went up on a ladder, after I fell in the brook, and I got red paint on my dress!"

"My, what a lot of things to happen!" murmured Mrs. Golden, as slowly and feebly she made her way around the store to the side where she kept the groceries.

"Let me get the pepper!" begged Bunny, as he saw the old woman looking toward a top shelf. "I can climb up."

"Well, my dear, if you're sure you won't fall, you may get it," said Mrs. Golden. "I've got some sort of a thing to reach down packages and boxes from the high shelf. My boy Philip got it for me. But I can hardly ever find it when I want it. Be careful now, Bunny."

"I will," said the little fellow, as he began to climb.

Sue watched her brother, thinking over what Mrs. Golden had told them about a legacy.

"If she got a lot of money," mused Sue, "she could get a big store, all spread out flat and she wouldn't have to have any high shelves. I hope she gets her legacy."

Bunny was just reaching for the box of pepper when there was a sudden barking of dogs outside the store and something black and furry, with a long tail, rushed in, leaped up on the counter, and thence to the top shelf, knocking down a lot of boxes and cans.

"Oh! Oh!" screamed Sue. "Look out, Bunny!"

CHAPTER XI

THE LAST DAY

Mrs. Golden was too surprised to do or say anything. She just stood still, looking up at Bunny. As for the little boy, he had been so startled that he almost let go his hold on one of the upright pieces of wood that held up the shelves. But he did not quite unclasp his hand, and so he clung there. Sue was dancing up and down in her excitement.

Then into the store rushed a big dog, barking and leaping about, his eyes fixed on that scrambling object in brown fur which had sprung to the highest shelf.

"Mercy me! What's that?" cried Mrs. Golden.

"It's Wango, Mr. Winkler's monkey," Sue answered.

And that is what it was.

Wango had got loose—nothing new for him—and had wandered out into the street. There a strange dog, catching sight of the animal, had chased him. Bunny and Sue knew it was a strange dog, for their own dog, Splash, and most other dogs in the neighborhood, were used to Wango and liked him. They seldom ran after him or barked at him. But this was a strange dog.

"GO ON OUT OF HERE!" SUE ORDERED.

"Go on out of here!" Sue ordered this dog. The animal stood looking from her to Wango on the high shelf, barking loudly now and then. "Go on out and let Wango alone!" Sue ordered.

The dog did not seem to want to go, however, and Mrs. Golden was getting a bit worried. She feared the monkey would leap about and knock down many things from her shelves.

"Wait a minute," called Bunny Brown. "I've got the pepper. I'll come down there and make the dog sneeze with it if he doesn't go out."

Bunny started to climb down, but there was no need for him to sprinkle pepper on the dog's nose to make him sneeze. For just as Bunny reached the floor in came Jed Winkler himself, looking for his pet monkey. Mr. Winkler drove out the strange dog, closed the door, and then coaxed Wango down from the high shelf.

"Did he do any damage, Mrs. Golden?" asked the old sailor. "If my monkey did any damage I'll pay for it."

"No, he didn't do any harm," she answered. "He just startled us all a little."

"Wango's a good monkey, but he will run away," said Mr. Winkler, petting his furry companion. "I'm glad he didn't do any damage. My sister said he'd be sure to this time, but I'm glad he didn't."

"He's a good climber," said Sue. "If you had a monkey, Mrs. Golden, he could reach things down from the high shelves for you, when your son goes off after leg-legacies."

"I'm afraid, dearie, that a monkey would be more bother than he was worth to me, just to lift things down off high shelves," laughed the old lady. "Wango is a lively chap, though."

"What's this about a legacy?" asked Mr. Winkler, for he was an old friend of Mrs. Golden.

"I don't count much on it," she answered. "Philip has gone to see about it. I got word that an uncle of mine had died and left some money and property. We may get a share of it and we may not."

"I hope you do!" exclaimed Mr. Winkler. "I most certainly hope you do!"

So did Bunny Brown and his sister Sue, for they were getting quite fond of Mrs. Golden, and liked to buy things at her store.

When the children were on their way home with the pepper, Mr. Winkler walking with them part of the way carrying Wango on his shoulder, Bunny said:

"When I keep a store like that I'm going to have a monkey to reach things down off the high shelves for me."

"He might get the wrong things," Sue objected.

"Maybe he would first," said Bunny. "But I'd train him. It would be fun to have a monkey in a store, wouldn't it, Sue?"

"Lots of fun!" agreed Sue.

"My goodness, children!" laughed Mary, as they entered the kitchen with the pepper, "it took you quite a while, and I was in a hurry. Didn't Mrs. Golden have any pepper?"

"Yes, but Wango got in the store," explained Bunny. "When I keep a store I'm going to keep a monkey, too!"

"Bless and save us, what does the child mean?" murmured Mary, but she did not stop for an answer, as she was in a hurry to get the supper on the table.

Some days after this, during which time Bunny Brown and his sister Sue had had much fun with their playmates keeping store and doing other things, the two children came down dressed to go to school. But they were singing and laughing in a way they seldom did unless something different was happening, or going to happen.

"Bless and save us!" exclaimed Mary, as she saw Bunny and Sue start out of the house hand in hand. "You're very joyful this morning. What's going on?"

"It's the last day of school!" explained Bunny, laughing still more.

"We'll have hardly any lessons," Sue added. "And when we come home to-day we don't have to go back to school for a long, long while. It'll be vacation!"

"Oh, so that's the reason!" laughed Mary. "No wonder you feel so pert and chipper—no school! Well, have a good time when you're young."

Bunny and Sue certainly had good times if ever children did.

As Sue had said, there were hardly any lessons at school that day. Reports were to be given out, little gifts were to be made to the teachers, and there were to be "exercises." That is, the pupils would recite or sing in their different classrooms.

Bunny and Sue were each to "speak a piece," and they had been preparing for some time, going over their recitations each night at home to make sure they would not forget and stumble and halt when they stood on the platform.

Miss Bradley was such a great favorite with her children that many had brought her little gifts.

These were placed on her desk, and then, after a few lessons, which no one took very seriously, Miss Bradley read the class a story. Then came the speaking of "pieces."

This was always one of the things that took place on the "last day," and was much enjoyed. No one had to recite unless he or she wanted to, and so no one was nervous or afraid, except about forgetting the lines.

Sadie West recited a verse about bees and flowers, and very pretty it was, too. Sue had picked out a funny verse about a little mouse, a trap, and a piece of cheese. I think most of you know it, so I'll not tell you about it.

Then came the turn of fat Bobbie Boomer. Bobbie was funny just to look at, and he was funnier when he got up to recite. He had picked out as his recitation that old, old poem about Mary and her lamb, for it was easy for him to remember that.

Now Bobbie had been very sure that he would not forget any of the verses when he got up on the platform. He had practiced his "piece" at home over and over until he knew it "by heart," and could almost say it in his sleep, his father remarked.

But when Bobbie got up on the platform and after he had made a funny, jerky, fat, little bow, all of a sudden every word of that poem seemed to slip from his mind! He stood there, looking around the room, now up at the ceiling and now down at the floor. His face grew red, and he began pulling at the buttons on his coat.

Miss Bradley felt sorry for him, and she laid her finger over her lips when she heard some of the children beginning to laugh.

"What is the name of your selection, Bobbie?" the teacher asked kindly.

"It—it's about Ma—Mary and her—her little lamb!"

"That's a cute little poem. Don't be afraid. I'll start you off, and then perhaps you can remember the rest. Now begin," and Miss Bradley said the first line.

This helped Bobbie very much, and he got along all right until he came to the verse about the lamb following Mary to school. Bobbie got as far as, "It followed her to school one day which was——"

And there poor Bobbie "stuck." He couldn't think what came next.

"It followed her to school one day—school one day—one day," he said slowly.

"Yes," said Miss Bradley kindly. "And what comes next, Bobbie? Was it right for the lamb to follow Mary to school?"

Miss Bradley wanted Bobbie to say, "which was against the rule," but Bobbie couldn't just then remember that. Suddenly his eyes opened wide. He pointed to the back of the room, where a clattering sound was heard, and cried:

"Look! Look what's coming in!"

CHAPTER XII

WATERING THE GARDEN

Instantly all the children turned around to look at what Bobbie Boomer was pointing to. And gasps of surprise came from Bunny Brown and Sue, as well as from the other pupils and the teacher.

For, standing in the doorway of the classroom, which was on the ground floor, was Toby, the Brown's Shetland pony. He stood there looking in, the wind blowing his fluffy mane and forelock, and his bright eyes looking around the classroom as if for a sight of Bunny and his sister.

"Oh, Toby!" cried Bunny. He had spoken out loud in school, but as it was the last day it did not so much matter.

"He came to school, just like Mary's lamb!" exclaimed Charlie Star.

Fat Bobbie Boomer seemed to be forgotten, but the sight of the pony appeared to have brought back to the little boy's mind the line he had missed.

"Which was against the rule!" he suddenly exclaimed.

Every one laughed, even Miss Bradley, and she added:

"Yes, it was against the rule for the lamb to follow Mary to school, and I suppose it's just as much against the rule for the pony to follow Bunny Brown and his sister Sue."

"Please, Teacher, he didn't follow me!" said Bunny.

"Nor me!" added Sue. "We didn't know he was coming! He was in the stable when we came from home."

This was very true, and they were all wondering how it had happened that Toby had followed the children. It was something he had never done before, and, though he was a great pet, he was not exactly Mary's lamb—he did not follow Bunny and Sue everywhere they went.

"Suppose, Bunny, you take Toby out of the room," suggested Miss Bradley, for the Shetland pony did not seem to want to go of his own accord. "Can you manage him?" the teacher asked.

"Oh, yes, I can ride home on his back, if you'll let me," said the little boy.

"School is almost over for the day, and also for the term," said the teacher with a smile. "You may be excused."

But Bunny did not have to leave. For just then in came Bunker Blue, the young man who worked for Mr. Brown at the fish and boat dock.

"Oh, you're in here, are you?" asked Bunker, speaking to Toby and taking hold of the thick mane of the little horse.

"Did he run away?" asked Bunny of Bunker. "Did he get out of his stall?"

"Not exactly," explained the tall young helper. "I was taking him down to the blacksmith shop to have new shoes put on him. I left him in front of the hardware store while I went in to get something for your father, Bunny, and when I came out Toby had slipped from his halter. I didn't know where he was until some one said they saw him come into the schoolhouse."

"He hasn't done any harm," remarked Miss Bradley.

"How did he get loose from the pony cart?" Sue asked.

"He wasn't hitched to the pony cart," answered Bunker Blue. "I was just leading him by the halter, but I guess I didn't have it strapped tight enough. Come along, Toby," he added. "I guess you've said your lessons," and the whole class, teacher and all, joined in the laugh which Bunker Blue started.

Toby whinnied, which was his way of laughing, I suppose, and then Bunker Blue led him forth from the classroom. So Bunny didn't have to leave school to ride his pet home, though I believe the little boy would have been very glad to do so—as would, in fact, any boy in the class.

"Well, now we will go on with our exercises," said Miss Bradley. "Can you remember your recitation now, Bobbie?"

The appearance of Toby seemed to have had a good effect, for Bobbie began again about Mary and her lamb, and gave all the verses, without forgetting a single line. Every one clapped his or her hands when he finished and made his bow.

In turn the other children recited. Then came the singing of some songs in which the whole school joined in the big assembly hall, and the "last day," ended.

"Now for the long vacation!" cried Bunny Brown, as he raced out of the schoolyard with the other boys.

"And lots of fun!" added Charlie Star.

"We'll go camping!" said George Watson.

"And sail boats!" added Harry Bentley.

The girls, too, were no less joyful. They talked of what they would do, of the play parties they would have and of picnics in the woods.

"Will you play store any more?" asked Mary Watson of Sue.

"Oh, I guess so," was the answer. "Bunny and I like that fun. Bunny wants to keep a real store when he grows up. Sometimes he lifts things down from the shelves for Mrs. Golden in her store."

Laughing, shouting, tagging each other, and running away, talking of what they would do during the long vacation, the school children ran on through the streets of Lakeport.

"Let's have a race!" cried Bunny.

"I can beat you!" declared Charlie Star.

Off they ran, feet fast flying, and Bunny was first to reach the hitching post in front of his house, this being the end of the race course for that particular time.

"Did Bunker Blue come back with Toby?" asked Bunny of his mother, after he had been given a piece of bread and sugar by Mary.

"No," was the answer. "But how did you know Bunker had Toby out? He didn't come for him until after you went to school," said Mrs. Brown.

"Oh, Toby came to school!" explained Sue, laughing.

"Toby came to school?" repeated her mother.

And then the story was told amid much laughter.

Just before supper Bunker Blue came back with Toby, and the children were allowed to hitch the Shetland pony to the basket cart.

"Do you want anything from the store?" asked Bunny, as he took his seat beside Sue and grasped the pony's reins.

"Better ask Mary," was the reply.

And, as it happened, Mary wanted some sugar.

"We'll get it at Mrs. Golden's," called Bunny, as he drove out of the yard.

"My, the children are getting fond of that old lady store keeper," mused Mary, as she went back to her kitchen work.

"I'm glad to have them," said Mrs. Brown. "It does children good to learn to be kind and thoughtful toward others. And, from what I hear, Mrs. Golden needs help. Her son works, but does not earn much, and she can't make a very good living from so small a store. We must buy what we can from her."

"Trust the children for that!" laughed Mary. "They'd run there all the while if we'd let them. Bunny was telling me Mrs. Golden had something the matter with one of her legs."

"Oh, no. He said she expected a legacy," explained Mrs. Brown. "That means she hopes to get a little property or some money from a relative who has died."

"Oh, I thought it was her legs, poor old lady!" said Mary. "Rheumatism, or something like that."

"Mrs. Golden isn't very well able to get around," admitted Mrs. Brown. "But that has nothing to do with a legacy."

Bunny and Sue drove up to the door of the little corner store.

"My, but you're coming in style!" exclaimed Mrs. Golden, when she saw them. "Are you going to buy me out?"

"No, we just want some sugar," said Bunny. "We're going to get five pounds, 'cause we can carry it in the pony cart."

"Yes, if it wasn't for the cart I'd be a bit afraid to give you so much as five pounds," said Mrs. Golden, as she went slowly behind the counter to weigh out the sweet stuff. "You might drop it. But it'll be safe in the pony cart. You'll be like a regular grocery delivery."

"Do you deliver things?" asked Sue.

"No, dearie. I can't afford to have a delivery wagon and a horse, to say nothing of one of those automobiles. And it wouldn't pay me to hire a boy, even when Philip is away. Sometimes he takes heavy things that are ordered, but mostly folks carry away what they buy. Let's see, now, how many pounds did you say, Bunny?"

"Five, Mrs. Golden. And please may I scoop it out of the barrel?"

"Well, yes, maybe; if you don't spill it."

"I won't spill any!" promised Bunny eagerly. "And may I put it on the scales? You see I'm going to keep a store when I grow up," he went on, "and I'll want to know how to weigh things on the scales."

"I hope you make more money than I do," sighed Mrs. Golden. "Now be careful of the scoop, dearie!"

Bunny felt quite proud of himself as he leaned down in the sugar barrel and dipped up the sweet, sparkling grains. Mrs. Golden guided his hands as he poured the sugar into the scoop of the scale, and of course she watched to make sure the weight was right, for Bunny was hardly old enough to know that.

But he did it nearly all himself, and he told his father so that evening after supper.

"My! I'll have to be on the lookout for a vacant place to rent so you and Sue can keep a store during vacation," replied Mr. Brown, laughing.

"Oh, we don't want to start a store unless Mrs. Golden gets her legacy so she'll be rich," declared Sue. "If we had a store she wouldn't sell so much and she'd be sorry."

"Well, maybe that's so," agreed her father, with a smile. "We'll wait until we find out about the legacy before we start you and Bunny in the store business. When will Mrs. Golden know about it?"

"When her son Philip comes back. He's gone to see about the legacy," said Bunny.

When they went to bed that night Bunny and Sue talked of what they would do during the long vacation. On account of some business matters, Mr. Brown could not take his family away that summer until about the middle of August. This left them with a good part of the vacation to spend in Bellemere, and the two children were beginning to plan for their fun.

One of the first things Bunny found to do the next morning—the first morning of the vacation—was to water the garden.

"May I take the hose and sprinkle?" he asked.

"If you don't get yourself wet through," his mother answered.

"I'll be careful," Bunny promised.

There was a vegetable garden at the side of the house, a garden which Uncle Tad had made and of which he was very proud. As there had been no rain for some days the garden was in need of water.

The hose was attached to the faucet, for Uncle Tad had been watering the garden the night before, and he had gone away, leaving word that if any one had time to spray more water on the vegetables they should do so, as the ground was very dry.

"I like to water the garden," said Bunny, and he took great delight in directing the stream from the hose over the cabbages, beets and potatoes which were coming up.

After watering for some time Bunny began to feel hungry, as he often did, and started in to ask Mary for some bread and jam. He laid the hose down, with the water still running, but he turned the stream so it would spray on the grass and not on the garden, so it would not wash out any of the growing things.

Bunny was coming out again, with a large slice of bread and jam, when from the front street he heard a man's voice crying:

"Here! Look out what you're doing! Be careful with that hose! You're soaking me!"

"Oh, oh!" cried Bunny Brown. "Sue must have picked up the hose that I left and squirted water on somebody!"

CHAPTER XIII

HELPING MRS. GOLDEN

Almost dropping his slice of bread and jam, so excited was he, Bunny Brown ran toward the hose. Before he reached it, for it was around the corner of the house, he heard the man's voice again calling out:

"Here! Stop that I say! Can't people go along the street without being wet with water from a hose? Pull your hose farther back!"

"Sue! Sue! Don't do that! Be careful! You're wetting some one," cried Bunny, as he ran along, not yet seeing the hose. But he could guess what had happened.

Sue, coming along and seeing the hose turned on, with the water spurting out, had picked up the nozzle end and was watering the garden. Only she held the hose so high that the water shot over the high front hedge and was wetting some man passing in the street.

That is what Bunny thought. But that is not what had happened.

Just before he turned the corner of the house he heard the man's voice once more saying:

"Say, isn't it enough to wet me once? What are you keeping it up for? I am trying to get out of the way, but you follow me. I'm coming in and see about this!"

Something very like trouble seemed about to happen.

"Sue! Sue!" cried Bunny, still thinking his sister was to blame. "Let that hose alone!"

But when he turned the corner of the house and could see the garden, Sue was not in sight. And, stranger still, no one was at the hose. There it lay, still spurting water out on the thick, green grass.

Who had picked up the nozzle and sprayed the unseen man in the street? If it was Sue where had she gone?

"Sue! Sue!" called Bunny. "Were you playing with the hose?"

Sue's head was thrust out of the window of her room upstairs.

"What's the matter, Bunny?" she asked.

"Oh, you're up there, are you?" exclaimed the little boy, much surprised. "Were you down here at the hose?"

"No. I'm getting dressed. I haven't been down in the yard at all yet."

"Then who did it?" thought Bunny. "I wonder——"

But just then a man, who seemed to have been out in a rain storm without an umbrella, came hurrying around the side path. He caught sight of Bunny standing near the hose.

"Look here, my little boy," said the man, trying not to speak angrily, though he was rightfully provoked, "you must be more careful with your hose. You have wet me very much. Does your mother know you are doing this?"

"She—she knows I'm watering the garden," Bunny answered.

"Does she know you were watering me?" asked the man, with a half smile.

"No—no, sir," replied the small boy. "I didn't wet you!"

"You didn't! Then who did?"

"I—I don't know," stammered Bunny. "I left the hose here while I went in to get some bread and jam. Here's some of it now," and he held out what was left of his slice. "I heard you calling, and I thought maybe it was my sister Sue. Course she wouldn't 'a' done it on purpose. But it wasn't Sue. She hasn't been downstairs yet."

"Then who was it?" insisted the man. "Surely the hose didn't wet me all by itself."

"No," admitted Bunny. "But it might have been Mr. Winkler's monkey."

"Who's Mr. Winkler's monkey, and how could he wet me with a hose?" demanded the man.

"His name is Wango—I mean the monkey's is," explained Bunny. "Sometimes he gets away and does things. He climbed up on Mrs. Golden's shelves—she keeps a store. Maybe Wango got loose and came over here and picked up the hose to get a drink or something, and so wet you."

"Well, that's possible," admitted the man. "And if that's the case I beg your pardon. Do you see Wango around here?" he went on, while Sue, looking from her upper window, wondered who the stranger could be.

"No, I don't see Wango," replied Bunny, looking about. "But I'll look for him. Maybe he's hiding."

"Maybe he is," and the man now laughed. "I'll help you search. For if the monkey is up to tricks like that he ought to be stopped. He may wet some one else if you go away and leave the water turned on."

"That's right," agreed Bunny.

He left the hose, still spurting, on the grass, and, followed by the man, walked around the yard, looking for Wango. But the mischievous monkey was not in sight, nor did he come when Bunny called, though Mr. Winkler's pet nearly always did this.

"I guess he isn't here," said Bunny at length. "But I didn't wet you with the hose."

"Then who——" began the man, but he stopped short to point and cry: "Look at that!"

As Bunny and the stranger were walking back toward the hose, Splash, the big dog, ran out from under the back porch and took hold of the hose in his teeth. He began to shake it as he often shook things with which he played.

"There!" laughed the man. "That's how I was sprayed! Your dog picked up the hose after you left it, and raised it high, so the water shot over the hedge and on me! Now the mystery is explained! It was the dog that did it!"

And so it was.

"Splash!" cried Bunny. "Drop that hose!"

Splash dropped it, and with a bark came running up to be petted. He did not know he had done wrong.

"I'm very sorry," said Bunny. "Splash, you're a bad dog!" he declared, and Splash drooped his tail between his legs.

"Oh, don't scold him," the man begged. "I like dogs, and I know they don't like to be scolded any more than we do—or than boys or girls do. It wasn't his fault. He thought the hose was left there for him to play with."

"Is anything wrong?" asked Mrs. Brown. Sue had told her mother about a strange man, all wet, in the yard talking to Bunny, and Mrs. Brown had come down to see about it.

"Just a little accident," explained the stranger. "I was passing in the street when it suddenly began to rain—or at least I thought at first it was rain. Then I knew it was some one using a hose and spraying me. I called to them, but that did no good, and I came in. I saw this little boy and the hose, and naturally thought he had wet me by accident. But it seems it was his dog," and he explained how it had happened.

"I am very sorry," apologized Mrs. Brown. "If there is anything I can do——"

"Oh, I will soon dry in the sun!" laughed the man. "I wasn't really angry, only I know children will get careless when they have a hose, and I was going to tell them to be more careful. But I don't suppose I can make Splash understand," and he patted the dog, whose tail was now wagging again.

"I'm glad you are so kind about it," said Mrs. Brown. "Bunny generally is careful when he waters the garden. If you will come in and get dry——"

"Oh, no, thank you! I'll dry better in the sun. Clean water will hurt no one, and I might just as well have been caught in a shower. Good-bye!" he called, and hurried away.

"After this, Bunny," advised his mother, as he kept on wetting the garden, "it will be best to turn off the water if you leave the hose."

"Yes, Mother, I will," he promised.

So that little happening passed off all right, and later Bunny and the gentleman—who was a newcomer in town, Mr. Halsted by name—became good friends.

One day, about a week after vacation had started, during which time Bunny and Sue had had much fun, the two children went to the little corner store kept by Mrs. Golden. Bunny and Sue each had two cents to spend, and they were allowed to get some candy.

As they entered the store they saw Mrs. Golden trying to sweep, but the way in which the old woman used the broom showed that she was in pain. As the children entered she stopped, held her hand to her side, and tried to stand up.

"Oh!" she murmured, in a low voice.

"Is it your rheumatism?" asked Bunny.

"That, or something worse," replied the old lady, with a sigh. "I get a pain in my side every time I sweep."

"Let me do it!" begged Sue. "I love to sweep, and I'd like to help you."

"So would I!" exclaimed Bunny. "I can sweep, too. Please let me!"

Almost before she realized it, Mrs. Golden had given up the broom to Sue, and the little girl was sweeping the store, while Bunny waited for his turn.

Suddenly the doorway was darkened, and a big man with a bushy black beard came stalking in.

"Where's Mrs. Golden?" he asked, looking at some papers in his hand. "I want to see Mrs. Golden," and his voice was cross.

"I'm Mrs. Golden," answered the old lady. "What can I do for you?"

"The best thing you can do is to pay that money!" snapped the man.

CHAPTER XIV

THE CROSS MAN

Bunny and Sue had at first paid no attention to the big man with the black beard who entered the little corner grocery store so suddenly. The children thought he was a customer come to buy some groceries.

But when the man, in that cross voice, said Mrs. Golden had better pay him some money, Bunny and Sue looked sharply at him, Sue holding on to the broom.

"'Cause I thought maybe he was a robber coming after Mrs. Golden's money," she explained later.

"What would you have done if he had been a robber?" asked Uncle Tad.

"I'd 'a' hit him with the broom," Sue replied.

"And I'd have helped her!" exclaimed Bunny.

But this was afterward. The man, however, as the children looked at him, did not appear to be a robber. He was big, and not very pleasant to look at, and his black beard was as bristling as some of those worn by moving-picture pirates. But he did not seem to be going to take any money from the cash drawer.

From the way poor Mrs. Golden looked, though, the children were sure the man had frightened her. She sank down in a chair, and stared silently at the man.

"Well!" exclaimed the cross man more crossly than at first, "I'm Mr. Flynt of the Grocery Supply Company. If you're Mrs. Golden, I want to know why you don't pay me that money?"

"I—I wish I could, Mr. Flynt," murmured the old lady store keeper. "I really thought I'd have it for you last week."

"But you didn't!" snapped out the man. "You told our agent who called two weeks ago that you'd have it last week. But you didn't pay it. Then you said you'd send it this week, and you didn't. Now I've come for it. You can't fool me!"

Truly, thought Bunny Brown and his sister Sue, no one could fool this man, nor play with him nor do anything with him except dislike him.

"Come, come, Mrs. Golden!" went on Mr. Flynt. "You owe us this money, you know, and you'll have to pay it!"

"If you'll only wait until my son Philip comes back," murmured the old lady, "he'll pay you some, I'm sure. He's gone away to get a little legacy, and if he gets it I'll have enough to pay you all I owe and more!"

"Yes, if he gets it!" sneered the cross man. "I've heard those stories before. But if your son doesn't get that legacy what then?"

"Oh, I'm sure he'll get it!" said Mrs. Golden, trying to smile. "But if—if he doesn't, why, I'll just have to owe you the money, that's all!"

"That isn't all!" exclaimed Mr. Flynt. "We've got to have money. We've been as easy on you as we could be. We've let your bill run a good deal longer than we do most folks' bills. You've got to pay your debts, just as we have to pay ours. Come now, I want some money!"

Bunny and Sue looked at each other. Both had the same thought. Sue dropped the broom and began feeling in her pocket beneath her handkerchief. Sue had only one pocket, and she was lucky, being a girl, to have that. Bunny had any number of pockets, and he was going through first one and then the other, finding different things in each—a top, pieces of string, his knife, odd bits of stone, a very black piece of licorice, and some nails. Bunny never knew when he might want some of these things.

"Here, Mrs. Golden!" exclaimed Sue, she being the first to get what she was after in her pocket. "Here's two cents I was going to spend for candy. You can have it to give to the man!"

"Bless your heart, dearie!" murmured Mrs. Golden, "I can't take your money."

"And here's my two cents!" exclaimed Bunny. "You can keep it. And you don't need to give us any candy either."

"No!" added Sue, though she had a catch in her breath as she said it, for she really wanted a bit of sweet stuff that day.

"No, no, my dear," said Mrs. Golden, trying to smile, though there were tears in her eyes. "Keep your money. I'll sell you some candy if you want it, but you mustn't give your pennies away. Anyhow, I must pay Mr. Flynt a great deal more than that."

"I should say so!" exclaimed the black-bearded man, though, somehow or other, his voice was not quite so cross as before. "Four cents wouldn't pay postage on the bills we have sent you!

"But now, Mrs. Golden," he went on, "I don't want to be any harder on you than I have to. If you're going to get some money in, or your son is, and you can pay us what you owe we won't sell you out."

"Sell me out!" cried the old lady. "Were you thinking of doing that?"

"We'll have to if you don't pay," was the answer. "You bought a lot of goods of us, and you must pay for them. If you don't we'll have to take these things away," and he looked around at the shelves of the store.

"If you take things away from her how can she sell them?" asked Bunny Brown.

"She can't," said Mr. Flynt. "But she must pay. Everybody must pay what they owe or be sold out. Now I'll give you a little more time," he went on. "I'll tell them, back at the office, that you expect a legacy, and when that comes you must pay."

"Yes, yes! I'll pay!" promised Mrs. Golden. "Only give me a little more time and I'll pay."

"Well, see that you do!" grumbled the black-bearded man, who appeared to be crosser than ever now. "When I come again I want money!"

He stalked out of the store with a scowl on his face, and Bunny and Sue looked first at each other and then at poor Mrs. Golden.

"I don't like that man!" declared Sue, as she picked up the broom.

"I don't, either!" said Bunny. "What makes him so cross, Mrs. Golden?"

"Maybe he can't help it, dearie. Going around making people pay up is a cross sort of work, I guess."

"But what makes him want you to give him money?" asked Sue. "I thought a store was a place where people paid you money. I didn't think you had to pay money out. Bunny's going to keep a store when he grows up. Will he have to pay out money?"

"No, I'm not going to!" cried the little boy. "People have got to pay me money, but I don't pay any."

"You have lots to learn about a store, little man!" said Mrs. Golden. "It isn't all fun, as you and Sue suppose. Do you see all these things on my shelves?" she asked.

The children looked around at them and nodded their heads.

"To get them I have to buy them from other people—from the wholesalers, as they are called," explained Mrs. Golden. "The Grocery Supply Company is one of them. I buy barrels of sugar, barrels of flour, big boxes of prunes, and so on, from this company. Then I sell a few pounds of sugar, flour or prunes at a time and make a little money each time I sell. You see I don't pay as much for the flour and sugar as I sell it for. The difference in price comes to me, and is what I live on, and sometimes it's little enough.

"And now the trouble is I have bought a great many things from this Mr. Flynt's company, and I haven't the money to pay for them. That's why he's cross. He has a right to his money, but I haven't it to give him."

"Why not?" Bunny asked.

"Well, because I don't sell very much in my little store. If I sold more I'd have the money to pay my bills."

"Oh, Bunny, I know what we can do!" cried Sue. "We can tell mother to buy everything here—all her groceries and things—and then Mrs. Golden will have money to pay the cross man."

"Your mother is very kind as it is," said the old lady. "I'd like to have her trade here, but of course I don't keep the best of everything. I have to sell cheap goods. But of course if I sold more of them I'd have more money and then I could pay my bills.

"But there, my dears, this isn't any fun for you. You came to get your pennies' worth of candy, and I'll pick it out for you. An old woman's troubles aren't for little ones like you."

"My father had troubles once," said Bunny, "and we hugged him and kissed him; didn't we, Sue? That was when there was a fire on his boat dock."

"Yes, we were sorry a lot," Sue replied. "And we're sorry for you now, Mrs. Golden, and I'm going to tell mother to buy all her things here."

"That's very kind of you," said the woman. "But if Philip only gets that legacy I'll have money enough to pay all my debts and a little left over. Now don't worry about me. Try to have a good time. I'll get your candy!"

"And I'll finish this sweeping," laughed Sue.

"I'll help," said Bunny Brown, and then, in spite of the cross man, there seemed to be a little bit of sunshine in Mrs. Golden's store.

CHAPTER XV

THE BROKEN WINDOW

"Daddy," said Bunny Brown that night, as the family were in the pleasant living room, "have you much money in the bank?"

"I have a little, Bunny, yes. But why do you ask?" Mr. Brown wanted to know.

"I have some in my bank!" cried Sue, before her brother could answer. "I guess maybe I have a hundred and seventy dollars!"

"Pennies you mean, dear! Pennies! Not dollars!" laughed her mother, for the children each had a penny bank.

"Well, pennies, then," agreed Sue. "But aren't a hundred and seventy pennies 'most the same as a hundred dollars?"

"Pooh! No!" said Bunny. "It takes a hundred pennies to make even one dollar!"

"Oh—o—o—! Does it?" exclaimed Sue. "What a terrible lot of money!"

"Yes, it does seem a lot," laughed Mr. Brown. "But why are you talking about money?" and he looked at his little son. "Why did you ask if I had any money in the bank?"

"I was wondering if Mrs. Golden had any in her bank," said Bunny.

"I don't believe she has very much," said Mr. Brown. "I was past her store to-day. It's a very small one. I don't see how she makes a living there."

"We were in there to-day," went on Bunny, "and a man came in and wanted a lot of money. He said Mrs. Golden owed him. He was from the grocery company."

"Yes, the wholesale house, I presume," remarked Mr. Brown. "Well, Bunny, did Mrs. Golden pay her bills?"

"No," said Bunny, a bit sadly, "she didn't. And Mr. Flynt was cross. I was thinking maybe if you had a lot of money in the bank you could take some out and give it to Mrs. Golden, and then she wouldn't have to cry when cross men came in. And she could pay you back when she got her leg—her legacy!" and Bunny brought the last word out with a jerk, for it was rather hard for him to remember.

"What's all this about?" asked Mr. Brown, looking at his wife in some surprise.

"I don't know," answered the children's mother. "It's the first I've heard of it. Bunny and Sue often go to the little corner store. It's handy when Mary wants something in a hurry."

"Tell me more about Mrs. Golden, Bunny," asked his father.

Thereupon the story of the cross man and the money the old lady owed to the grocery company was told as well as the children could tell it.

"It's too bad!" exclaimed Mrs. Brown. "I want you children to be as kind as you possibly can to Mrs. Golden. Help her all you can, Bunny and Sue."

"And will you buy things there?" asked Sue.

"Why, yes," agreed her mother. "We will trade there all we can. Mr. Gordon, the big grocer, can afford to lose a little of our custom."

"Do you think you could give her any money out of your bank, Daddy?" asked Bunny. "And she could give it back after she got her legacy."

"I'll see about it," was the smiling answer. "I know some of the men in the Grocery Supply Company," went on Mr. Brown, "and I'll ask them to be a bit easy with the old lady. But you didn't tell us about this legacy, Bunny. You told us about the cross man, but not about the legacy."

"The children have spoken of it to me several times," said Mrs. Brown. "It seems some relative of Mrs. Golden has died, and her son has gone to see about some money or property that may come to his mother."

"She'll have plenty of money when she gets her legacy," remarked Bunny. "She told me so."

"Then let us hope that she gets it," said Mr. Brown. "And now don't you children worry any more about it," he told Bunny and Sue. "I'll help Mrs. Golden if she really needs it."

"And we'll help her, too," said Bunny to his sister, as they went to bed that night.

"Hey, Bunny! Hi, Bunny Brown!" called a voice under Bunny's window early the next morning.

"Hello! Who's down there?" Bunny asked, jumping out of bed.

"Come on down!" cried Charlie Star. "We're going to have a ball game! We're waiting for you! Bobbie Boomer, Harry Bentley, George Watson, and all the fellows are over in the lots waiting. Come on have a ball game!"

"I didn't know it was so late!" murmured Bunny, rubbing his eyes. "I'll be right down!"

He had, indeed, slept later than usual, and as this was vacation time, his mother had not called him, though Sue had got up and had gone off to play with some of the girls.

Bunny had his breakfast and then he ran over to the big lots with Charlie. A number of boys were tossing and batting balls, and when Bunny arrived there were enough to make up two "sides" and have a game. Bunny was captain of one team and Charlie Star of the other.

"Now, fellows, we want to beat!" cried Bunny, as he took his place to pitch the first ball of the game.

"Yes! Ho! Ho! I'd like to see your side win!" laughed Charlie. "We won't let you get a single run!"

It was all jolly good fun, and though each side tried to win it was in good-nature, which is how all games should be played. First Bunny's team was ahead, and then Charlie's, until it came close to noon, when the boys knew they would have to stop playing and go home to dinner.

"Now, fellows," said Bunny Brown, as it was his turn to bat, "I'm going to knock a home run and that will win the game for us!"

"Pooh! You can't knock a home run!" laughed Charlie, who was pitching for his side.

Bunny swung hard at the ball which Charlie pitched to him. And Bunny himself was a little surprised when his bat struck it squarely and the ball sailed away, much farther than he had ever knocked a ball before.

"Run, everybody! Run!" cried Bunny Brown, dropping the bat and starting for first base himself. Two of his side were on the other bases, and if they could all get in on his home run it would mean that his side would win.

Higher and higher and farther and farther sailed the ball Bunny had knocked, away over the head of fat Bobbie Boomer, who was playing out in center field. It surely was going to be a home run.

"Oh, look where that ball's going!" cried Charlie Star, turning to watch it. "Oh, it's going to break one of Mr. Morrison's windows!" Mr. Morrison was a rather crabbed, cross old man who had a house on the edge of the vacant lots where the boys played ball.

Bunny was too excited over his home run to pay much attention to where the ball went, and Tom Case and Jerry Bond, who were running "home," thought only of how fast they could run. But the others watched the ball, and a moment later saw it crash through one of Mr. Morrison's windows.

By this time Bunny was at third base. He did not stop there, but ran on in, touched home plate, and sank down to rest, very tired but happy because he was sure his side would now win the ball game.

Out in the field, near the fence that was around Mr. Morrison's house, Bobbie Boomer was calling:

"I can't get the ball! I can't get the ball! It's in Mr. Morrison's house!"

And, surely enough, that's where it was—right in the house. It had gone through the window.

"I—I made the home run all right!" panted Bunny Brown. "I told you I would, Charlie Star!"

Bunny had run so fast that he had not heard the tinkle of the breaking glass, nor had he seen where his ball went.

"Yes, you made a home run all right!" yelled Charlie. "And now we'd better all run home or Old Morrison will be after us for busting his window. Come on, fellows! Let's run home!"

The game was practically over, and a number of the boys, fearing the anger of Mr. Morrison, started after Charlie, running away from the lots. But this was not Bunny Brown's way.

"Did I—did the ball I batted break a window?" he asked.

"You ought to 'a' heard the crash!" panted Bobbie Boomer, running in from center field. "Old Morrison will be here in a minute! You'd better run, Bunny!"

Surely enough, a moment or two later Mr. Morrison came out on his back porch, from which he could look into the lots. He saw the boys, some of them running away. In his hand he held the baseball that had crashed through his window.

"Hi, there!" he cried. "Who did this?"

One or two boys, seeing that Bunny was not going to run, had stayed with him.

"Who did this?" cried Mr. Morrison again.

Up spoke Bunny Brown, walking toward the angry man.

"I—I knocked the ball," he said.

"Well, you broke my window, young man, and you've got to pay for it!"

"I—I will!" faltered Bunny. "I have some money in my bank, and if you come home with me I'll take it out and pay you."

Mr. Morrison seemed surprised at this. In times past when his windows were broken the boys had run away, or, if they had not, they had been saucy to him and had refused to pay for any glass. This was something new.

"What's your name?" asked Mr. Morrison.

"Bunny Brown," was the answer.

"Does your father keep the boat dock where Bunker Blue works?"

"Yes, Sir."

"Oh," said Mr. Morrison, not so angry now. "Well, of course this window has to be paid for, but I know your father, Bunny Brown. He and I do business together. And Bunker Blue does me favors once in a while. I guess there won't be any hurry about paying for this glass. You can pay me five cents a week if you want to. And I should think the other boys ought to chip in and help you pay for it. That's what we used to do when I played ball. If a window was broken we all helped pay for it."

"I'll help," offered one boy.

"So will I!" said another.

By this time Charlie Star and the boys who had started to run away began straggling back. They wondered why Bunny and his companions were not being chased by Mr. Morrison. And when Charlie and his chums heard about the offer to pay shares for the broken glass Charlie said:

"I'll pay my part, too!"

"So will I!" cried his players.

"That's more like it," chuckled Mr. Morrison, and, somehow or other, the boys began wondering why they had ever called him cross. Certainly he seemed quite different now. Perhaps it was the way Bunny had acted, so bravely, that made the change.

"Now look here, boys," went on the uncross Mr. Morrison. "I know you have to play ball, and this isn't the first time you have broken my windows. But it's the first time any of you have had the nerve to stay here and offer to pay. I like that. And now that you all offer to chip in and pay for it, it'll not be too hard for any one boy. It's the right spirit. And I want to say that if you always do that there'll not be any trouble.

"Not that I want any more windows broken," he added, with a laugh. "But if they are smashed, chip in and pay for them. And now I'll have the pane of glass put in and you can take up a collection among yourselves and pay me later on. I'm in no hurry as long as you act fair.

"And now if you'll come in here I think maybe I can find something that you boys would like to have," he added. "Don't be afraid, come on in," he invited, opening a gate in his side fence.

The boys hesitated a moment, and then, led by Bunny Brown, they entered. What could Mr. Morrison have in mind?

They soon found out. He led them down into the cellar and showed them some old baseballs, some bats, some gloves, and, best of all, a good catcher's mask.

"Here are some old baseball things," said Mr. Morrison. "I got them in a lot of junk I bought a year ago, and I've been wondering what to do with them. I like the way you boys acted—especially some of you," and he looked at Bunny. "I'm going to let you have these things for your team," he said. "But try not to break any more of my windows!" he laughed.

"We won't!" promised Bunny Brown. "Or, if we do, we'll pay for 'em!"

"Crackie! What dandy stuff!" cried Bobbie Boomer.

"Now we can have regular league games!" exclaimed Charlie Star, who was perhaps the best player of all the boys.

"And a real mask, like the Pirates have!" cried Harry Bentley.

"Take 'em along," said Mr. Morrison. "They're only cluttering up my cellar. I'm glad to get rid of 'em, and especially to good boys."

"We—we were afraid of you at first," said Charlie.

"Well, you needn't be any more," chuckled Mr. Morrison. "Just pay for my window, when you get the money together, and we'll call it square!"

Talking, laughing gleefully, and wondering at their good fortune, the boys hurried from the cellar. And they had another game that same afternoon, with the balls, bats, gloves and mask that Mr. Morrison had given them. Only Bunny knocked no more home runs, and Charlie's team won, which was, perhaps, as it ought to be. And, best of all, no more windows were broken.

It was quite an adventure for Bunny Brown, but it was not the last he and his sister Sue were to have, for many good times were ahead of them for the long vacation.

CHAPTER XVI

LITTLE STOREKEEPERS

"Here, Bunny! Here, Sue!" called Mrs. Brown, one bright, sunny morning. "Where are you?"

"We're coming, Mother!" answered Bunny.

He and his sister were playing in the yard down near the brook. Bunny had carried to the brook a little boat, and Sue had with her one of her very small dolls which was having a voyage on the small vessel. She had picked out a celluloid doll.

"'Cause then if she falls off into the water it won't hurt if she gets wet," said Sue.

"That's right!" agreed Bunny.

But now the children left their play and ran to see what their mother wanted.

Before doing so, however, Bunny made fast the little boat to a tree on the bank of the brook, tying it by a long string. And Sue took the celluloid doll off the deck and laid her on the grass in the shade.

"'Cause she might go off sailing by herself," Sue explained.

"Pooh! She couldn't sail my boat!" laughed Bunny.

"Well, she might," said Sue.

Then they ran to their mother—who was waiting for them on the back steps.

"What do you want, Mother?" asked Sue.

"Is it time to eat?" is what Bunny Brown asked. Bunny, like many children, was always ready for this.

"No, it isn't time for lunch," laughed Mrs. Brown. "But I want you to bring some things from the store so Mary can get lunch ready. And this is a chance for you to help your friend Mrs. Golden."

"What do you mean—help her?" asked Bunny. "Is daddy going to give her some money out of his bank so she can pay the cross man?"

"I don't know about that," replied Mrs. Brown. "But I mean you can help her now by getting some groceries from her. The more we buy and the more other families buy, the more money she will make, and then she can pay her bills."

"That's so!" exclaimed Bunny. "I'm going to ask all the fellows to buy their things of Mrs. Golden instead of going to Gordon's."

"And I'll ask the girls!" exclaimed Sue.

"We mustn't desert Mr. Gordon altogether," said Mrs. Brown. "He wants to do business, too. But Mrs. Golden needs our trade most, I guess, so get these things of her. I've written them down on a paper so you'll not forget, and as there are a number of them you had better take a basket, Bunny."

"I will," he said. "Do we have to hurry back, Mother?" he asked.

"Oh, there is no special hurry," his mother answered. "But what did you want to do? Play another game of ball and break another window?" and she smiled at Bunny, for she had heard the story. Mr. Morrison's window had been paid for by all the boys "chipping in," or clubbing together.

"I'm not going to play ball," said Bunny. "But Sue and I might stay with Mrs. Golden a little while and help her in the store if you weren't in a hurry."

"No, I'm not in a hurry," Mrs. Brown said. "Help Mrs. Golden all you can, poor old lady!"

Together Bunny and Sue went around the corner to the little grocery and notion store. They were talking of what they might do to help the storekeeper, and they were planning what fun they could have with the little boat and doll when they reached home again. By this time they were at the store, but, to their surprise, the front door was closed, though this was summer, and it generally stood wide open.

And in one corner of the door was a piece of paper on which something was written. Bunny and Sue saw this notice and they at once guessed that something had happened.

"Maybe she's gone away with her son Philip to get the leg-legacy!" exclaimed Bunny.

"Maybe," said Sue. "Go on, Bunny, you can read better'n I can. Read what it says."

Slowly Bunny read the little notice on the front door. It said:

"Please come to the side door."

Wonderingly the children went along the path to the side door, for the grocery of Mrs. Golden was in an old-fashioned house which had been built over so she could sell things in it. The side door was almost closed, but, though open a small crack, Bunny and Sue did not want to push it open further and go in. Instead they knocked.

"Yes? What is it? Who's there?" called the voice of Mrs. Golden. It was a weak, quavering old voice.

"We're here," answered the little boy. "Bunny Brown and his sister Sue!"

"Oh, my dears! I'm glad it's you and not Mr. Flynt!" said Mrs. Golden. "Push the door open and come in. I have such a dreadful headache that I couldn't keep the store open. I had to come to my room back here and lie down. I just had to close the store!"

The children entered to see their friend lying on a sofa in the room back of the store. She had her head tied in a rag.

"Are you very sick?" asked Sue.

"'Cause if you are I'll go for the doctor," offered Bunny.

"Oh, no, thank you, my dears, I'm not ill enough for that," answered Mrs. Golden. "Just a bad sick-headache. I'll be better to-morrow. But I couldn't keep the store open to-day."

"That's too bad," said Bunny. "We came to get some things," and he took out the list his mother had written for him.

"Well, I want to sell things, but I am too ill to get up and wait on you," said the storekeeper. "I put that sign in the front door so if any wholesale wagons came to leave stuff they could find me. But, really, I don't feel able to get up."

Then Bunny had an idea.

"Couldn't Sue and I wait on ourselves?" he asked eagerly. "We want to get these things here, and if you told me where to find them—though I know where to find some myself—and if you told me how much they were, I could pay you, and it would be all right. I have the money."

"Yes, you might do that," said Mrs. Golden. "It would be fine if you could. Now let me see what you want, and then see if you can get it from the shelves."

"I can climb like anything!" said Bunny gleefully.

"Well, don't fall!" cautioned Mrs. Golden. Together, with the help of their friend, Bunny and Sue picked out from the closed store the things their mother had written on the list for them to get. Mrs. Golden told them where certain groceries were kept, and the price.

"Why, you are regular little storekeepers!" declared Mrs. Golden, trying not to think of her aching head. "You have waited on yourselves as well as I could have done."

"I wish we could wait on some regular customers!" boldly exclaimed Bunny.

"Wouldn't it be fun!" laughed Sue.

There came a knock on the side door, and a woman's voice called:

"Are you there, Mrs. Golden? I want a few things. May I come in?"

"Oh, yes, come in, Mrs. Clark," replied the storekeeper, as she recognized the voice of one of her customers. "If I can't wait on you you can help yourself, as Bunny and Sue did."

A woman came in the side door.

"Let us wait on you, please!" begged Bunny. "My sister and I can get what you want."

"Why, yes, I guess you can!" agreed Mrs. Clark, with a laugh. "I want a yeast cake and some sugar. It's too bad you two children couldn't stay and help Mrs. Golden," she added, as Bunny and Sue brought what she wanted and she was giving the money to the store owner.

"We'd love to stay!" cried Bunny.

"And we can, for a while," added Sue. "Mother said we didn't have to hurry."

"Oh, could we open the front door and tend store for you really?" asked Bunny, his eyes sparkling in delight.

CHAPTER XVII

TWO LETTERS

Mrs. Golden thought it over for a minute. Really, with her head aching as it did, she was in almost too much pain to think, but she felt that something must be done. She needed all the money she could take in, and if customers were turned away from her store, because the door was closed, she would lose trade. Not many would come around to the side as Mrs. Clark had done.

"Couldn't we tend store for you—a little while?" asked Bunny again, as he saw Mrs. Golden thinking, as his mother sometimes thought, when he or Sue asked her if they might do something.

"We could ask you where things are that we don't know about," added Sue, "and we wouldn't talk loud or make a noise."

"Bless your hearts, dearies!" sighed Mrs. Golden. "You are very kind; but I'm sure I don't know what to say."

"Then let me say it," advised Mrs. Clark. "I say let the children tend store for you, Mrs. Golden. Bunny and Sue are a lot smarter for their age than most children. You let them tend store for you, and I'll run over once in a while to see if everything is all right."

"Very well," said Mrs. Golden. "You may keep store for me, Bunny and Sue."

"Goodie!" exclaimed Sue, clapping her hands. Then she happened to remember that she must not make too much noise, and she grew quieter.

"I'll open the front door and take down the sign," said Bunny. "We'll wait on the customers for you, Mrs. Golden."

Bunny felt quite like a grown man as he removed the card and turned the lock in the front door, swinging it open. The shades had been pulled down over the show windows, and Bunny and Sue now ran these up.

"I'll run along now," said Mrs. Clark, going out the front door and nodding in friendly fashion at the children. "I guess you'll make out all right, and I'll be back in a little while. If she gets any worse, or anything happens, just come and tell me—you know where I live," she said in a low voice, so Mrs. Golden, in the back room, would not hear.

Sue nodded and Bunny smiled. They were rather anxious for Mrs. Clark to go, so they would be left in charge of the store. And when this happened, when really, for the first time, Bunny Brown and his sister Sue were truly storekeepers you can hardly imagine how pleased they were.

"You go to sleep now, Mrs. Golden," said Sue, going on tiptoe to the rear room, to look at the old woman lying on the couch. "You go to sleep. Bunny and I will tend store."

Then she went back to Bunny, who sat on a stool behind the grocery counter. He had decided he would sell things from that side of the store, while Sue could wait on the dry-goods and notions side.

"All we want now is some customers," remarked the little boy.

"Yes," agreed Sue. "We want to sell things."

They waited some little time, for the corner store was not in a busy part of town. Several times, as footsteps were heard outside, Bunny and Sue hardly breathed, hoping some one would come in to buy. But each time they were disappointed.

Finally, however, just when they were about to give up, thinking they would have to go home, a woman came in and looked around, not at first seeing any one.

"What can I do for you to-day, lady?" asked Bunny Brown, as he had often heard Mr. Gordon say.

"Oh, are you tending store?" the lady asked. She was a stranger to Bunny and Sue.

"Yes'm, I and my sister—I mean my sister and I—are keeping store for Mrs. Golden. She's sick," said Bunny. "I can get you anything you want."

"All I want is a loaf of bread," the lady answered.

Bunny knew where to get this, and also the kind the lady wanted, as it was the same sort of loaf his mother often sent him for. He put it in a paper bag and took the money. The lady gave the right change, so Bunny did not have to trouble Mrs. Golden.

All this while Sue stood on her side of the Store, rather anxiously waiting. She wished the customer would buy of her.

"You are rather small to be in a store, aren't you?" asked the lady, as she started to leave with the bread.

"Oh, we know lots about stores," said Bunny. "We often play keep one, but this is the first time we ever did it regular."

"I know how to keep store, too," said Sue, unable to keep still any longer. "Would you like some needles and thread?"

"Yes, now that you speak of it, I remember I do need some thread, my dear," the lady answered, with a smile. "Can you get me the kind I want?"

"I—I guess so," Sue answered, yet she was a bit doubtful, as there were so many things among the notions.

"Well, perhaps I can help you," said the lady. "I see the tray of spools of silk right behind you, and if you'll pull it out I'll pick the shade I want. I have a sample of dress goods here."

SUE HELPED HER CUSTOMER MATCH HER SAMPLE.

Sue had often been with her mother when Mrs. Brown matched sewing silk in this way, and the little girl pulled out the shallow drawer of small spools. She saw the sample and knew the lady needed red sewing silk; so she at once pulled out the right drawer. Then she helped the customer match her sample until she had what she wanted.

"How much is it?" asked the lady, taking out her purse.

Here was Sue's trouble—she did not know exactly, and she did not want to go ask Mrs. Golden, for the storekeeper might be sleeping. To call her might make her head suddenly ache worse.

"I generally pay ten cents a spool," said the customer, "and I suppose that's what it is here. If it's any more I can stop in the next time I pass. That is, unless you can find out for sure."

"Oh, I guess ten cents is all right," said Sue, and she found out later that it was.

Then the lady left with her bread and thread. The children had waited on their first customer all alone.

In the next hour, during which the children remained in the store, they waited on several customers, and did it very well, too, not having to ask Mrs. Golden about anything, for which they were glad. Of course the things they sold were simple articles, easy to find, and of such small price that the men or women who bought them had the right change all ready.

Once a boy came in, and you should have seen how surprised he was when Bunny waited on him. He was Tommy Shadder, a boy Bunny knew slightly.

"Huh! you workin' here?" asked Tommy, as he took the sugar Bunny put in a bag, not having spilled very much.

"Sure, I'm working here!" declared Bunny. "That is, for a while," he added, for he knew he would soon have to go home.

"Huh!" said Tommy again, as he went out. "Huh!"

"Mail!" suddenly called a voice, and the postman entered the store. "Where's Mrs. Golden?" he asked, as he saw Bunny and Sue, whom he knew.

"She's got a headache, and we're tending store," Sue answered proudly.

"Oh, all right. Here's a couple of letters for her. She's been asking me for letters all week, and I didn't have any for her. Now here are two."

He tossed them on the counter and went out into the sunlit street. Bunny looked at the two letters.

"Oh!" he exclaimed. "One's from Mrs. Golden's son Philip. Maybe it's about the legacy!" Bunny had seen the name Philip Golden in the corner of the envelope.

"Who's the other from?" asked Sue.

"The Grocery Supply Company," read the little boy from the other envelope.

"Oh, dear!" sighed Sue.

"What's the matter?" asked Bunny.

"Maybe that's a bill," Sue said, for she had often been in her father's office on the dock when the mail came in, and when he received a thin letter Mr. Brown would hold it up to the light, laugh, and say:

"I guess this is a bill."

Sue knew what bills were, all right, and she seemed to feel that bills coming to Mrs. Golden, who had little money, would be worse than those which came to her father's office, for Mr. Brown never seemed to worry about the bills.

As the children looked at the letters on the counter, wondering whether or not to take them in to Mrs. Golden, she herself came out of the back room. She looked at the children and then at the letters.

"Oh, some mail!" she exclaimed. "I hope it's from Philip about the legacy! If it is, I'm sure it will completely cure my headache, which is much better."

Eagerly Bunny and Sue watched to see Mrs. Golden open the letters.

CHAPTER XVIII

BUNNY HAS AN IDEA

Mrs. Golden read first the letter from her son, sent to her from the distant city. But if Bunny and Sue thought to see a look of joy spread over the store owner's face they were disappointed.

"Did he—did your son send you the legacy?" asked Bunny, as the letter was folded and put back in the envelope.

"Well, no, not exactly," was the answer. "It seems there is some trouble about it. I hoped Philip could come home to help me, but he can't, and it will be some time before we'll get any money from that legacy—if we ever get it. Oh, dear! So many troubles!"

Mrs. Golden sighed and opened the other letter. Her troubles seemed to be more now, for she sighed again as she laid this letter aside. Sue could not help asking:

"Is it a bill?"

"Something like that, yes," answered the old lady. "It's from Mr. Flynt's grocery company. It says if I don't pay soon I'll be sold out."

Mrs. Golden sighed again. The children did not know exactly what it was all about, but they knew there was trouble of some kind and they wanted to help. But they felt, too, that it was time they went home.

Mrs. Golden must have seen the worried looks on their faces, for she tried to smile through the clouds of her own trouble as she said:

"Never mind, my dears! Run along now, for I'm sure your mother will be getting anxious about you. You have been a great help to me. I guess I'll find some way out of my troubles—I hope so, anyhow. Run along now! It was good of you to help me."

So Bunny and Sue, taking the things they had bought, started out of the store.

"If she could only sell more things she'd have more money and then she could pay that grocery bill," said Bunny to his sister.

"Yes," agreed Sue. "We'll tell daddy about it and see what he says. Daddy has lots of money."

"But maybe he needs it," suggested Bunny. And very likely Mr. Brown did.

However, children of the ages of Bunny and Sue are not unhappy for very long at a time, and trouble seems to roll away from them like water off a duck's back. On the way home they met some of their playmates, and in talking over a picnic that was to be held in a few days Bunny and Sue forgot about Mrs. Golden for a while.

"You stayed rather a long time," said Mrs. Brown, when Bunny and Sue finally reached home with the groceries she had sent them for.

"You said we could stay," said Bunny.

"And we helped Mrs. Golden by tending store," added Sue.

"Did you really tend store?" Uncle Tad asked, and he was much surprised when the children told what they had done.

"I guess she doesn't do much business," remarked Uncle Tad. "She has a store on a corner, which is the best place for one, as people on two streets pass it. But I'm afraid she isn't enough of a hustler."

"What's a hustler?" asked Bunny, wondering if Mrs. Golden might be made into one.

"A hustler," said Uncle Tad, "is a person that does things in a hurry. Some storekeepers are hustlers for business. If business doesn't come to them they go after it. That's how they sell things."

"How could Mrs. Golden sell more things?" Bunny questioned. "She's got lots of things in her store—heaps and packs of 'em—but she doesn't sell much."

"That's the trouble!" said Uncle Tad. "She doesn't advertise, and she doesn't make any window display."

"What's a window display?" Sue inquired.

"I saw you looking at one the other day," replied the old soldier. "Do you remember when I passed you and Bunny while you were looking in the drug store window on Main Street?"

"Oh, yes! Where the rubber bags were!" cried Bunny.

"A little doll was making believe swim in a rubber bag," said Sue, "and there was a big crowd looking at it."

"That's it!" exclaimed Uncle Tad. "That drug store man got a big crowd in front of his store by putting something in the window that made people stop and look. That's advertising."

"Maybe Mrs. Golden could fix up her windows so a crowd would stop in front!" exclaimed Sue.

"What good would that do?" Bunny asked. "She wants people to come inside her store and buy things."

"That's it," agreed Uncle Tad. "But if you get a crowd outside a store, because there's something to look at in the windows, some of that crowd will go inside and buy something."

"Only Mrs. Golden hasn't any rubber bags," went on Bunny. "But I guess Sue could lend her a doll if she wanted it to take a swim."

"Mrs. Golden doesn't need to put rubber bags in her window," said Uncle Tad. "That wouldn't be the thing for a grocery and notion store. She should put in something that people would stop to look at, or have a special sale or something like that. And another thing I've noticed, when I've been past her place is that the windows are very dirty. You can hardly see what's inside. If her windows were cleaned and she had something in them, a crowd would stop and more people would go in and buy than go in now. Mrs. Golden needs to advertise in that way."

Uncle Tad went out. Mrs. Brown busied herself about the house, and Bunny Brown motioned to his sister Sue to come to the side porch.

"What you want?" asked Sue.

Bunny put his finger over his lips.

"I've got an idea!" he said. "I know how we can help Mrs. Golden get a crowd in front of her store."

CHAPTER XIX

THE WINDOW DISPLAY

Bunny Brown and his sister Sue spent much time during the next few days out in their barn—that is when they were not going to the store for their mother. Every chance they had, however, they bought things of Mrs. Golden, to help her as much as they could by trading at her store.

"And we ought to get the other boys and girls to go there," Sue said.

"We will, after a while," agreed Bunny. "Just now we have to do something else."

And the something else had to do with his idea and the time he and Sue spent in the barn. With them, most of the time, was Splash, their dog, and Charlie Star often came over with a covered basket.

"What do you think the children are doing?" asked Mrs. Brown of Mary, the cook, one day.

"Oh, I guess they're getting up some kind of a show," Mary answered. "I can hear Splash barking now and then, and there's a cat mewing."

"Cat!" exclaimed Mrs. Brown. "We haven't a cat!"

"I guess it's Charlie Star's," went on the cook. "He brings it over every day in a basket and takes it home again. I guess they're getting ready for a show."

"Bunny and Sue did have a show once," observed Mrs. Brown. "I hardly believe they would get up another. I must see what they are up to."

However, as company came just then and Mrs. Brown had to entertain them, she forgot all about her two children. Meanwhile things were happening out in the barn.

But Bunny and Sue kept it a secret, in which only Charlie Star had a share, and Charlie did not tell. When Mrs. Brown's company had left some one telephoned to her and she forgot all about her plan to ask Bunny what was going on.

It was a few days after this that Bunny and Sue were again sent to the store for their mother, and you may easily guess to which store they went—the little corner one, of course.

Mrs. Golden was sitting in her usual easy chair, and there were no other customers in the place.

"How's business?" asked Bunny, as he had often heard men ask his father.

"It might be better and not hurt itself," was Mrs. Golden's answer. "Customers are few and far between."

"Mrs. Golden," said Bunny, "my Uncle Tad says you ought to have a special sale. Did you ever have one?"

"Oh, yes, years ago," she answered. "I had a sale of notions, and a number of women came in to get things to make dresses with. But I haven't had a special sale for a long while."

"Why don't you, then?" asked Bunny eagerly. "I think a special grocery sale would be good. You could put a lot of things in your window and mark the prices on them, and people would come in to buy."

"Yes, I suppose I could do that," agreed Mrs. Golden slowly. "I have a big stock of a new kind of oatmeal on hand. Some new concern sold it to me, but it didn't take very well. Lately I got a letter from them saying I could sell it at a special price. I suppose that would bring in some trade. I never thought of it. I'm getting too old, I guess, and worrying too much. When my son Philip comes home I'll have a special sale."

"No, don't wait!" cried Bunny Brown eagerly. "Let's have it now! Where are those oatmeal things?"

Mrs. Golden smiled at his eager, bustling air.

"They're in the storeroom," she said. "Some of the cases aren't open yet."

"We'll open 'em for you!" cried Bunny. "Then we'll stack the oatmeal in the window, and we'll make a sign saying it's awful cheap and you'll sell a lot, Mrs. Golden."

"Well, maybe I will, dearie. I'm sure I hope so. And it's good of you to help me. Let me see now, I'll put 'em in the left window, I guess. That has less in it," and she looked toward the window she meant. So did Bunny and Sue, and Sue's first idea was made plain when she said:

"Could I wash that window, Mrs. Golden?"

"Wash the window? Why, yes, I suppose so," answered the storekeeper. "It is pretty dirty," she added. "I don't very often look at 'em, and that's a fact. I declare! you can hardly see what I have in my windows, can you? Dear me, I am getting old. If Philip was here he'd wash 'em for me."

"I'll do it!" offered Sue. "I often wash the low windows for mother. She lets me. Have you got any of that white stuff that makes 'em shine?"

"Oh, yes, I know what you mean," said Mrs. Golden. "Yes, you can take a cake from the grocery shelf. My, I never thought of a special sale and having windows washed. It may bring me trade!"

"Uncle Tad says it will!" exclaimed Bunny. In a measure it was Uncle Tad's idea that Bunny and Sue were carrying out.

"You wash the window," he told his sister, "and I'll open the oatmeal."

Soon there was a busy time in Mrs. Golden's store. Bunny was hammering and pounding away opening the oatmeal cases, and Sue was washing the window, having first taken out the few things Mrs. Golden had on display there—not that you could see them very well from the outside, however.

"Could I wash the other window, too?" asked Sue, when she had finished the first.

"Are you going to put oatmeal in both windows?" asked Mrs. Golden. "Seems to me that will be too much. Wash the other window if you want to, dearie, but two of them filled with oatmeal——"

"Oh, we aren't going to put oatmeal in both!" exclaimed Bunny, with a queer look at his sister. "We're going to fix up the second window to make people come in and buy."

Mrs. Golden did not seem to understand exactly. She shook her head in a puzzled way and murmured that she was getting old.

And as the postman came along just then with a letter from Philip, she was soon so busy reading it that she paid little attention to what Bunny and Sue were doing.

The children worked hard and faithfully all morning, and promised to come back in the afternoon. When they left to go home to lunch, both windows were brightly shining, though there were a few streaks here and there where Sue had forgotten to wipe off the white, cleaning powder. But they didn't matter.

"I'll pull the shades down," said Bunny, as he was leaving. "We don't want people looking in the windows until we get 'em all fixed up, and then we'll surprise 'em."

"Just as you like, dearie. Just as you like," said Mrs. Golden, in a dreamy tone. She was thinking of what her son had said in his letter.

Hurrying through their lunch as quickly as their mother would let them, Bunny and Sue hastened back to Mrs. Golden's store. They told something of their plans at home, and Uncle Tad said:

"That's a fine idea! I'll stop down there later and see how it looks."

"Come on, Splash!" called Bunny to his dog, as he and his sister started back. "We want you!"

"And we must stop at Charlie's house and tell him," said Sue.

"Yes, we will," Bunny agreed, and Charlie, when he heard the news, said:

"I'll be at the store in about half an hour."

Certainly things were getting ready to happen.

Bunny and Sue found Mrs. Golden lying down on her couch in the back room when they reached the store again.

"I'm afraid I have another of my bad headaches coming on," she said.

"You lie down," said Sue kindly. "Bunny and I will tend store again, and we'll start the special sale."

The windows were now dry and clean. All the old goods had been taken out, and Bunny and his sister were ready to put in the special display of oatmeal which was to be sold at a low price. Mrs. Golden told Bunny where to find some price cards to put in the window telling of the special sale. These cards were of a sort that most grocers keep on hand.

With the help of Sue, Bunny piled the boxes of oatmeal in the window. They were stacked up as nearly like a fort as he could make them, and he knew how to do this, for he had often helped the boys build forts of snow. Here and there he left holes in the piled-up wall of oatmeal boxes.

"Oh, if you only had something like little cannons to put in the holes it would look more like a real fort!" said Sue.

Bunny thought this was a good idea, and looked around for something to use. He saw some round pasteboard boxes, the top covers of which were a dull black.

"They'll look just like cannons," he said, as he fitted them in the holes of the oatmeal box fort. The window shades being down, no one could see from the street what was going on. Splash, the big dog, was content to sleep in the store while the children were there.

"Now for the other window," said Bunny to Sue, when the oatmeal was all in place, with the low price plainly marked on cards stuck here and there.

"We have to wait for Charlie," Sue said.

"He's coming now," observed Bunny, looking from the door. No customers had come in while the children were busy fixing the window, and they were just as well satisfied. They hoped for a rush of trade when the shades were raised.

Charlie came in with the covered basket, and the next fifteen minutes were busy ones for the children. Mrs. Golden had fallen asleep and did not come out of the back room to see what they were doing.

"Well, we're all ready now," said Bunny, at last. "Pull up the shades!"

He and Charlie did this. The sun shone in through the newly cleaned windows and lit up such a display as never before had been seen in Mrs. Golden's store.

CHAPTER XX

IN THE FLOUR BARREL

Slowly the heavy green shades, which hid what was in the cleaned windows from the sight of persons in the street, rolled up. Bunny Brown, his sister Sue, and Charlie Star waited for what was to happen next. They looked first at one of the windows in which they had made a display, and then at the other.

In one was the pile of oatmeal packages built up like a small fort, with holes here and there through which stuck round boxes, with black covers so that they seemed to be small cannon.

In the other window—but I can best tell you what was in that by telling you what happened.

The curtains had not been up very long, and the children were feeling rather proud of what they had done, especially Sue in making the glass so clean, when a boy who was passing along the street stopped to look in one of the windows.

And the window he looked at was not the one where the oatmeal boxes were piled. It was at the other. This boy was soon joined by a second. Then a girl who had been running, as if in a hurry, came to a stop, and she stood near the two boys, looking in.

"The crowd is beginning to come!" remarked Charlie Star.

"But they aren't buying any of the oatmeal," objected Sue.

"Never mind," Charlie went on. "These kids wouldn't buy anything anyhow; they haven't any money. Wait till the big folks come." Charlie spoke of the "kids" as if he were about twenty years old himself. He seemed to have become much bigger and more important since helping Bunny and Sue fix up Mrs. Golden's windows.

And, surely enough, a few minutes later men and women began to stop to look at the windows of the little corner store. And the men and women at first looked not at the oatmeal but at the other window.

"It's making a big hit!" said Bunny Brown. He had learned this saying at the time when he and his sister Sue gave a show.

By this time quite a crowd had gathered in the street outside, and there was some talk and laughter which was heard inside the store. It was even heard in the back room where Mrs. Golden had gone to lie down, and it aroused her from her doze.

"Well, children," she said, as she came slowly out, "have you got the windows washed, and the special sale of oatmeal started?"

"Yes, everything is all ready," answered Bunny, with a sly look at his sister and Charlie.

Then Mrs. Golden saw the crowd outside.

"My goodness!" she exclaimed. "I never knew oatmeal to be so popular. I can sell it all, maybe!" Then she noticed that the crowd was mostly looking at the other window.

"What have you in there, Bunny Brown?" she asked.

"Take a look and see," invited Sue.

Mrs. Golden peered over the wooden partition that fenced the show window off from the remainder of the store. And in the window she saw—what do you think? Well, I imagine you must have guessed by this time.

Yes, it was Splash, the big dog, and asleep on his back was Charlie Star's little white kitten! It made the cutest picture you can imagine, for Splash kept very still, as if he did not want to wake up the sleeping puss, and the little cat was curled up just as if on a silken cushion.

It was this that Bunny and Charlie had been planning in the barn for several days. At first Splash would have nothing to do with the white kitten, and the kitten fluffed up her tail and made funny noises at Splash.

But finally the boys and Sue had trained the two to be friends, so that Splash would lie down and allow the kitten to go to sleep on his back. And it was this that Bunny and Sue, together with Charlie Star, had planned to attract attention to Mrs. Golden's poor little store.

The children had succeeded better than they had dared dream. Outside the crowd was getting larger and larger all the while, and men were saying:

"That's a pretty good dog!"

The women said:

"What a pretty picture!"

Little girls said:

"I wish I had that pussy!"

The boys wished they owned Splash. Many of them knew him, for they had often seen the dog with Bunny Brown. But the kitten was new, and few knew that Charlie Star owned it.

And then happened just what Uncle Tad had told the children would take place if they could draw a crowd outside the store. Some began to look at the special display of oatmeal in the other window, and a few came in to buy. Some bought not only oatmeal but other things as well, happening to remember that they were needed at home.

Mrs. Golden, who felt much better after her sleep, was kept very busy waiting on customers, and Bunny and Sue helped her, as did Charlie.

SPLASH AND THE KITTEN DID THEIR SHARE IN DRAWING TRADE.

Splash and the kitten did their share, too, in drawing trade. For soon the kitten awakened and began playing with a spool which Charlie had hung up on a string in the window. The little white cat struck at the spool with her paws as she stood up on the back of the big dog. Splash did not seem to mind it in the least. In fact, he looked as if he enjoyed it, and this amused the crowd all the more.

"Well, I do declare! You children beat anything I ever saw!" exclaimed Mrs. Golden, when she had time to look and see what was going on in the special display window. "You've made my store into a regular circus!"

"But it's good for business, isn't it?" asked Bunny.

"Indeed it is!" said the old lady, with a smile. "I never was so busy. That oatmeal is selling fine. I wish I'd had a special sale of it before."

Besides the boxes in the window there were packages of oatmeal piled on shelves ready to be sold. And as the price was lower than oatmeal could be bought for at other stores, Mrs. Golden did a good trade.

After a while things became a little quieter in the store, after the first surprise had worn off. But now people were constantly passing in the street, and many of them stopped to look at the dog and cat, which were now playing together, Splash gently pawing at the white kitten which climbed all over him.

Bunny had just finished selling a man a package of oatmeal, and Sue was getting out a paper of pins for a lady when Uncle Tad came into the store.

"Hello, children!" he cried in his jolly way. "I see you took some of my advice and advertised by your show windows," he added to Mrs. Golden.

"Bunny and Sue did it for me," she said, "with the help of Charlie Star. It is wonderful."

"If you'll get me a white piece of cardboard and a pen and some ink I'll make you a sign to put in that oatmeal window," offered the old soldier. "Those signs are all right, Bunny," said Uncle Tad. "But for a special sale you want a special sign. Let me see now," he went on, as Mrs. Golden got him what he had asked for. "You have made those oatmeal boxes into the shape of a fort with guns. Now I must make a sign to go with it. Let me see. Ah, I have it!"

He was busy with the ink for several minutes, and then he held up a sign which read:

FORT-IFY YOUR CONSTITUTION
WITH THIS OATMEAL

"There!" exclaimed Uncle Tad, "this ought to bring more customers!"

"Ha! Ha!" laughed Mrs. Golden. "That's a pretty good joke!"

Bunny, Sue, and Charlie could not see anything funny, or like a joke, in the sign. But then it was not intended for children, so it did not matter.

But men and women passing in the street and pausing to read what Uncle Tad had printed, seemed to think it was odd, for they stopped, read it, laughed or chuckled, and then either passed on or came in and bought some oatmeal. And quite a few came in, so that by night Mrs. Golden had sold nearly all of the cereal.

"My goodness!" she said, when it was time for Bunny, Sue, and Charlie to go home. "This has been a wonderful day. Could you come over to-morrow?" she asked. "I don't mean to work," she added quickly. "For I'm afraid your mothers will think you're doing too much for me. But I mean could you come over and bring your dog and cat to put in the window. They certainly brought the crowd."

"Yes, we'll bring Splash," said Bunny.

"And I'll bring my kitten," offered Charlie.

"And we'll come and help you sell things!" laughed Sue. "We like it, don't we?" she asked the boys, and of course they said they did.

The first attempt of Bunny and Sue to advertise Mrs. Golden's store had been very successful. Of course Uncle Tad had told them how to do it, and Charlie Star had helped by bringing his kitten and training her with Bunny and Sue. So the special oatmeal sale made quite a bit of talk in that section of Bellemere near the little corner store.

Of course Mrs. Golden did not make a great deal of money, for the profit on each thing she sold, even the many boxes of oatmeal, was small. But it brought new customers to her store, and she was well pleased with what had happened.

"And if Philip can only get that legacy," she murmured to herself that night, "things will be easier for me. But I owe a lot of money to Mr. Flynt, and I don't know where I'm going to get it to pay—not even if those dear children help me with a lot more special sales, bless their hearts! Well, I'll do the best I can."

The next day Bunny, Sue, and Charlie again came to Mrs. Golden's store. Charlie could not stay, however, as he had to rake up the leaves around his home, but he brought his kitten, and again the dog and the white pussy drew crowds to the store window.

Besides oatmeal Mrs. Golden also had a special sale on notions, and she did a fairly good business in them, so that she and Sue were kept busy behind the counter. Not that Sue could do as much as Mrs. Golden, but she did all she could.

Bunny waited on some customers who came in to buy groceries, and when one lady wanted some flour an accident happened. Bunny was leaning over to scoop the white stuff out of the barrel, and as it was near the bottom he had to stand up on a box to reach it.

Suddenly the lady on whom he was waiting, and who was watching him, gave a startled cry.

"What's the matter?" asked Mrs. Golden.

"That little boy has fallen into the flour barrel!" was the answer.

CHAPTER XXI

SUE COULDN'T STOP IT

There was a banging, kicking sound and several cries of "Oh, dear!" The cries were faint and muffled, as if they came from the cellar. Then the lady who had ordered three pounds of flour, which Bunny was trying to scoop out for her, ran behind the counter.

Sue followed. So did Mrs. Golden. All they saw were Bunny's heels sticking out of the barrel, waving in the air, and now and then banging against a low shelf near which the flour barrel stood.

"Oh, dear! Oh, dear!" cried Bunny, from inside the barrel.

For that is where he was. He had fallen into the flour barrel!

"Pull him out!" begged Sue.

"I can't. I'm not strong enough to pull him up!" panted the customer, but doing her best.

"We must all pull!" exclaimed Sue. "Bunny pulled me out of the brook, and I'll pull him out of the flour barrel!"

"Yes, we must all pull!" said Mrs. Golden.

Together they all grasped Bunny by the heels and lifted him out of the flour barrel.

Oh, but he was a queer sight! Luckily he had stuck out his two hands when he felt himself falling head first into the nearly empty barrel, and had landed on his outstretched palms. And as there was not much flour in the barrel his head had not gone into the fluffy white stuff, or he might nearly have smothered. As it was his face was completely covered with the white particles.

And when Mrs. Golden, the customer and Sue had pulled the little boy from the barrel, and set him on his feet, Sue could not help laughing.

"Oh, Bunny!" she cried, giggling. "You look—you look just like the clown in the circus!"

And truly Bunny did, for his face was plastered as white as the face of any funny man that ever made jokes beneath the canvas.

"You poor boy," said the customer.

"Oh, Bunny, I'm so sorry!" exclaimed Mrs. Golden.

"I—I'm all right," declared Bunny, blowing out a white cloud of flour as he talked. "I—I didn't spill any!"

"No, you spilled yourself more than anything else," said Mrs. Golden. "I guess I'd better get the flour, Bunny, after we brush you off. It's too low in the barrel for you to reach. I don't want you falling in again."

"All right," agreed Bunny. "I guess I'm not quite big enough for flour barrels."

He was dusted off out in the side yard, so no great harm resulted from his accidental dive into the barrel, and Mrs. Golden waited on the flour customer.

"What did you think, Bunny, when you were falling into the flour barrel?" asked Sue, when the excitement was over and business was going on as before in the little corner store.

"What did I think?" he repeated. "Why, I guess I didn't have time to think anything. I just felt myself slipping, and then I fell in. I stuck out my hands, and I'm glad the flour wasn't deep in the barrel."

"It was like the time when I fell into the brook!" said Sue, with a little laugh. "Only I fell in feet first and you went in head first."

"Yes," laughed Bunny, "I went in head first all right!"

Mrs. Golden told the children they must not try to do things that were too hard for them, even though they meant to be kind and help her.

The second day of the special sale of oatmeal and notions was not quite as busy as the first. The novelty of the cat and dog in the window wore off and Bunny brought some of the little pet alligators to show. Still quite a number of people came in to buy, and Mrs. Golden was well pleased, thanking Bunny, Sue, and Charlie many times. She also wanted to thank Splash and the white kitten and the best way to do this was to feed them, which she did, as well as the alligators.

"We'll come and help you tend store to-morrow," said Bunny as he and Sue went home that night, Sue carrying Charlie's kitten in a basket and Splash following at Bunny's heels. The alligators were left till next day.

"I'm afraid your mother will think you are doing too much for me," said the old lady, as she said good-bye.

"Oh, no!" exclaimed Bunny. "She told us to help you all we could."

"And we like it!" Sue exclaimed. "It's fun."

"Except when you fall into flour barrels!" added Bunny Brown, with a laugh at some white spots that still clung to his jacket.

Mrs. Brown did not mind how much Bunny and his sister helped Mrs. Golden, but she told the children they must not stay in the store too much.

"Your long vacation from school is given you so you may play out in the sunshine and fresh air," said Mother Brown. "And though it is all right for you to help Mrs. Golden in her store, I want you to have some fun also."

"It's fun in the store," said Bunny.

"Well, I mean other kinds of fun," added Mrs. Brown.

So there were days when Bunny and Sue only went to Mrs. Golden's grocery on some errand for their mother or Mary, but even on these short trips they often were able to help the storekeeper, sometimes making little sales, if she was busy in another part of the house, or by arranging goods on the shelves.

Having learned that she could do more business by having her windows clean and with things nicely piled in them, Mrs. Golden kept this plan up, Bunny and Charlie and Sue often stacking goods where they would show well.

But with all this even the children could see that Mrs. Golden was worried. Bunny often saw her adding up figures on bits of paper, and she would look at the sum and sigh.

"What's the matter?" Bunny once asked.

"Oh, I owe so much money I'm afraid I'll never be able to pay," she said. "And it seems to be getting worse, even with all the help you children give me. If only Philip would get that legacy!"

"Hasn't he got it yet?" asked Bunny.

"No, not yet," was the answer. "And I'm afraid he never will. I miss him so, too. If he were here to help me things might go easier. But there! I mustn't complain. I'm much better off than lots of folks!" she added, trying to be cheerful.

"If more people would come to buy here you'd have more money," said the little boy. And that gave him an idea that he did not speak about just then, but turned over and over in his busy little head.

Heeding their mother's advice, Bunny and Sue played out of doors with their boy and girl chums, sometimes going on picnics and excursions or on walks through the woods and over the fields. Bunny and Charlie often played at boats in the brook, and more than once they fell in. Sue and her friends often waded in the water of the brook.

Bunny did not again, though, topple into any flour barrels. It was Sue who had the next accident at the corner grocery, and this is the way it happened.

The little girl had been sent by her mother to get a yeast cake at Mrs. Golden's, and when Sue reached the store she found the old lady busy with two women who were matching sewing silk. At the same time a little boy had come in for some molasses.

"I'll get the molasses for you," Sue offered, for she knew where the barrel was kept, and once Mrs. Golden had allowed her to raise the handle of the spigot and let the thick, sticky stuff run out into the quart measure. Sue was sure she could do this again. So, taking the boy's pail, she went to the molasses barrel.

It was kept in the back part of the store, and perhaps if Mrs. Golden had seen what Sue was about to do she would have stopped the little girl. But the two customers were very particular about the sewing silk they wanted, and kept Mrs. Golden busy pulling out different trays.

Sue reached the molasses barrel, set the quart measure under the spout, as she had seen Mrs. Golden do, and raised the handle. The next thing the storekeeper knew was when Sue came running up to her in great alarm crying:

"I can't stop it! I can't stop it!"

"Can't stop what, my dear?" asked Mrs. Golden.

"I can't stop the molasses from running out!" cried Sue. "I got it turned on, but I can't turn it off, and it's running all over the floor!"

"Oh, my goodness!" cried Mrs. Golden, hurrying to the back of the store.

CHAPTER XXII

A SHOWER OF BOXES

Sister Sue, as soon as she had told Mrs. Golden what had happened also started to run back to the molasses barrel. In fact she ran ahead of the storekeeper, and Sue's hurry was the cause of another accident.

For the molasses, running out of the spigot which Sue had not been able to close, had overflowed the quart measure, and was now spreading itself out in a sticky pool on the floor.

It was a slippery puddle, as well as a sticky one, and Sue's feet, landing in it as she ran, slid out from under her.

Bang! she came to the floor with a thud.

"Oh, my dear little girl!" cried one of the customers, who had been buying the sewing silk. "Are you hurt, child?"

Sue, sitting in the molasses puddle—yes, she was actually sitting in it now—looked up, thought about the matter for a moment, and then answered, saying:

"No, thank you, I'm not hurt. But I'm stuck fast. I can't get up."

It was very sticky molasses.

Mrs. Golden, thinking more about the waste of her precious molasses than about Sue for the moment, reached over and shut off the spigot. It had caught and was hard to close, which was why Sue could not do it.

Fortunately, however, the little girl had nearly closed it before the quart measure was quite full, and not so much of the molasses had run out on the floor as might have if the spigot had been wide open all the while. But, as it was, there was enough to make Sue fall, and to hold her there in the sticky mess after she had sat down so hard.

"Dear me, what a mess!" exclaimed one of the customers.

"Isn't it!" said the other.

"I—I'm awful sorry," faltered Sue. "My father will pay for the molasses I let run out, Mrs. Golden!"

"Oh, don't worry about that," said the old lady, though she was a bit worried over the loss, for nearly a pint of the sweet stuff had run away. "It's you I'm thinking of," she said. "Are you sure you aren't hurt?"

"No," answered Sue. "But my dress is. Oh, how am I going to get home?" she went on, as she pulled up the edge of her skirt and saw how dirty and sticky it was.

"You'll have to get into the bath tub, clothes and all," said one of the customers.

"It's like when I fell in the brook," half sobbed Sue.

"There, never mind!" said Mrs. Golden kindly. "Here, little boy," she said, reaching over and lifting up the brimming measure of sweet stuff, "take your molasses and run along. Then I'll clean up here."

Leaning over, to keep her feet out of the puddle, Mrs. Golden helped Sue to rise, though it was a bit hard on account of the sticky molasses. Then the little girl's dress was taken off and she was sent into Mrs. Golden's bedroom.

"I'll wash this dress and your petticoat out for you, Sue," said Mrs. Golden, when her thread customers were gone. "But it will hardly be dry for you to wear home before dark."

"If you should see Bunny, you could send him home to get another dress for me," Sue suggested.

"Yes, I could do that," agreed Mrs. Golden. "I'll see if Bunny is coming after I put your clothes to soak."

But Bunny was off playing ball that day, and did not come to the corner store. However, fat Bobbie Boomer happened to pass, and Mrs. Golden sent him to Sue's house.

He rather frightened Mrs. Brown at first, for Bobbie twisted the message and said Sue had fallen into a barrel of molasses, instead of just into a puddle on the floor, so that Mrs. Brown came hurrying to the store, imagining all sorts of things had happened.

She had to laugh when she heard the real story, and then she went back to get a clean dress for Sue, leaving the other to be washed and dried by Mrs. Golden.

"I'm afraid the children are more of a bother to you than a help," said Mrs. Brown, as she started home with Sue.

"Oh, bless their hearts, I don't know what I'd do without them!" said the storekeeper. "They are a great help. My store business is much better than before they began coming here. That special oatmeal sale brought me new customers, and Bunny and Sue are a great help."

As it would be rather hard work for Mrs. Golden to clean up the sticky puddle, Mrs. Brown sent Bunker Blue up from the boat dock to help. For this Mrs. Golden was very glad, as she could hardly have handled the broom and pails of water as well as Bunker did.

"This is easier than cleaning out boats," declared the fish boy as he "swabbed" the floor, as he called it.

Soon the store was scrubbed nice and clean and ready for more customers the next day. As Bunny and Sue had nothing special to do they went to the corner grocery to see if they could do anything to help. And Sue was told by her mother to bring home the washed dress and petticoat.

"We've come to help," Sue announced, as she entered the store. "But I'm not to draw any more molasses! Mother said I wasn't to!"

"Well, perhaps it will be as well for me to do that," said Mrs. Golden, with a smile. "That spigot is sometimes hard to close."

"And I'm not to dip up any more flour," added Bunny.

"Yes, I suppose it will be as well for me to do that, too," said the storekeeper. "But since you like to help me tend store there are many other things you can do."

Bunny and Sue found them, for it was afternoon now, and many families in the neighborhood sent children to buy things for supper.

"Hello, Sue!" called George Watson as he came into the store, whistling. "I told my mother about that special sale of oatmeal you had here last week. Got any more?"

"Yes, a few boxes left," said Mrs. Golden, who was behind the grocery counter with Sue. Bunny was out in the storeroom opening a new box of prunes. "They're up on a high shelf, I'll get one down for you, Sue."

But as she was going to do this a man entered the store. He was Mr. Flynt, and Sue heard Mrs. Golden sigh when she saw him.

"You'll have to wait a minute about that oatmeal," said the storekeeper to George. "I'll get it down for you in a little while. I have to see this gentleman first."

George was willing to wait, but Sue was anxious to help in the store, and as she saw that Mrs. Golden was going to be busy talking to Mr. Flynt, the little girl decided she could get down the box of oatmeal herself. She felt sure that Mrs. Golden would have trouble with Mr. Flynt who would want money, and Mrs. Golden had very little to pay.

"I'll get the box of oatmeal for you, George," said Sue. "I know where it is."

She climbed up on the counter by means of a box, and stretched up her little hands and arms to the shelf on which the cereal was stacked. Sue reached for a box, managing to get hold of it by stretching as far as she could and standing on her tiptoes. But as she pulled the one box out it caught on several others standing in line on the shelf.

"Look out!" cried George, as he saw what was going to happen.

But it was too late. Sue could not get out of the way, and a moment later a shower of pasteboard boxes of oatmeal and other things fell all around her.

"What is happening?" cried Mrs. Golden, hearing the clattering sound. She came hurrying from the back of the store where she had gone to talk quietly to Mr. Flynt.

"Everything is going to fall!" cried George.

But it was not quite so bad as this. Sue kept her hands raised above her so nothing would hit her head, though one or two boxes did bump her a little.

Box after box slipped from the shelf, falling on the floor, on the counter, and all around poor little Sue!

CHAPTER XXIII

THE PONY EXPRESS

Bunny Brown ran out of the storeroom, in his hand a hammer with which he had been opening the box of prunes. Mrs. Golden gave a cry of alarm as she heard the clatter of the boxes falling around Sue. Mr. Flynt joined Bunny in a rush to help the little girl. As for George, he was so frightened by the sudden toppling of things from the shelf that a tune he had started to whistle died away and he got ready to run out of the store.

"Mercy sakes! what is going on in here?" cried Mrs. Clark, entering the store as the boxes ceased falling. "Is anybody hurt?"

No one knew for a moment, as Sue had uttered no cry save the first frightened one. But by the time Bunny and Mr. Flynt reached her the shower of boxes was over and the little girl took down her hands from over her head.

"Did anything break?" asked Sue, looking about her. "Oh, dear, what a terrible mess!" she cried.

"Don't worry about that, child!" exclaimed Mrs. Golden. "What if a few boxes are broken open? It's you I'm thinking of."

"Oh, I'm all right!" Sue said, and she laughed a little.

And when they came to look her over nothing worse had happened than that she had a few bumps and bruises. And they were not very hard ones, for the boxes were of pasteboard and not wood.

And only one or two of the oatmeal packages were split open, so that not much was lost in that way. So, take it all in all, the accident was a very little one, though it made a great deal of excitement for the time being.

"You oughtn't to reach up for such high things, little girl," said Mr. Flynt, when he had helped pick up the packages.

"No, sir, I guess I oughtn't," agreed Sue. "But George wanted one and I thought I could get it."

"You call me when you want things from a high shelf," said Bunny, going back to the task of opening the box of prunes. "I'm a good climber."

"I wasn't climbing, I was reaching," answered Sue, as if that made a lot of difference. "Here's your oatmeal, George," she added, and the whistling boy came back to the counter and got it.

Bunny and Sue stayed in the store for an hour or more after the fall of the oatmeal boxes. Bunny finished opening the box of prunes, and he and Sue waited on several customers, for Mrs. Golden seemed to be quite busy talking to Mr. Flynt in the back room. And it was not a pleasant talk, either, as Bunny and Sue guessed when they caught glimpses now and then of Mrs. Golden wiping tears from her eyes.

Finally the grocery man came out of the back room with Mrs. Golden. He was saying, so that the children could hear:

"Now you'd better take my advice, Mrs. Golden, and sell out your store here. You'll never make it pay, and you keep on owing us more money all the while. I know you're trying to do your best, but you must either pay us or we'll have to take our things back and sell you out besides for the rest that you owe us.

"Take my advice and sell out before you're sold out. It will be better that way. We can't wait any longer. This is a good little store, but you don't make it pay."

"Maybe I could if my son Philip were to come back," sadly said the old lady. "He's gone after a legacy, and when he comes back——"

"There there, Mrs. Golden! It's of no use to talk that way!" exclaimed Mr. Flynt. "You've been telling me about that legacy a long time. Why doesn't it come?"

"I don't know, Sir."

"No. And I don't believe it ever will come. We've waited as long as we ought, but I'll give you a little more time, and that will be the last. If you don't pay we'll have to close your store. Think it over and sell out before you're sold out."

And then Mr. Flynt went out.

Bunny and Sue, who had been about to go home, looked at Mrs. Golden and felt sorry for her. They could see that she was feeling bad, and that she had been crying.

"What's the matter?" asked Bunny.

"Not enough money—that's the trouble," was her answer. "Oh, dear, I don't want to sell my store!" she said. "I want to keep it."

"Have you got to sell?" asked Sue.

"Mr. Flynt says so," came the reply, "because I owe him a lot of money I can't pay. If business was only better I might keep my store going until Philip comes back with the legacy. Once we get that we'll be all right! But if we don't——"

Mrs. Golden put her handkerchief to her eyes. Then, seeing that she was making Bunny and Sue sad, she added:

"There now! Run along. Maybe I can get the money somehow. At any rate you children have been most kind to me. Run along now, and don't mind a poor old woman."

But Bunny and Sue did mind. They talked matters over on their way home and decided that something must be done. They wanted to help more than they had been doing, and Bunny thought of a way. As usual Sue agreed with him, for she was willing to do anything her brother did.

That evening after supper Bunny brought his little tin savings bank from a shelf in his room, and Sue brought hers. There was a great rattling as the pennies, dimes and nickels in the tin boxes clattered against the sides.

"My goodness! what's going on?" cried Daddy Brown, looking up from the paper he was reading. "Are you two going to buy an automobile with all that money?"

"Will you please open my bank, Daddy, and see how much is in it?" asked Bunny.

His father, wondering what was "in the wind," as old Jed Winkler would say, did so. With Bunny's help the cash was counted. There was eight dollars and fifteen cents.

"I have more than that!" exclaimed Sue, and indeed she had, for Bunny had taken some of his money the week before to buy a top and a set of kite sticks. Sue had ten dollars and forty-six cents in her bank.

"What are you going to do with it?" asked Mrs. Brown, for she knew the children would not have gotten down their banks unless they had some plan in their heads.

"We're going to give it to Mrs. Golden," said Bunny.

"Mrs. Golden?" cried their father.

"You mean you're going to buy something at her store?" asked Mrs. Brown.

"No, we're going to give it to her," said Bunny gravely. "She owes money and Mr. Flynt will close up her store if she doesn't pay. So we're going to give her our money so she can pay Mr. Flynt and then the store will stay open."

"'Cause if it's closed," added Sue, "we can't have any more fun helping keep it."

"Oh, ho! I see!" laughed Mr. Brown. "Well, I must admit I forgot all about Mrs. Golden. I promised to see if I couldn't help her when you told me about Mr. Flynt before, but I forgot. Now, children, it wouldn't be right for you to take your bank money to help Mrs. Golden. She wouldn't want you to do that. Put away your pennies, and I'll see what I can do to help."

This made Bunny and Sue feel happier, and they went to bed more satisfied, for they felt sure their father could make everything right. But the next day, when they went in to see Mrs. Golden, to help keep store, they found her looking very sad and unhappy.

"What's the matter?" asked Sue.

"Oh, just the same old trouble," Mrs. Golden answered. "I need money to pay bills."

"Mr. Flynt's?" asked Bunny.

"Yes, his and another man's. I'm afraid, children, you won't be able to come here much longer and help keep store."

"Why not?" Bunny wanted to know.

"Because there won't be any store—at least I won't have it. I'm afraid I'm going to lose it. If I could only get some more customers and do more business I might manage to pull through until Philip gets back. But I don't know—I don't know!" and she shook her head sadly.

That afternoon, going home with Sue, Bunny had another idea.

"Sue!" he exclaimed, "if we can't give our money to Mrs. Golden maybe we can get her more customers."

"How?" asked the little girl.

"We can ask everybody we know to come and trade there," said Bunny. "I remember when the Italian shoemaker started down at the end of our street and I took my rubber boots there to have him fix a hole, he said for me to tell all the boys I knew to bring their boots and shoes to him to be mended."

"Did you?" Sue inquired.

"Yes. And the shoeman said I brought him good trade and he gave me a piece of beeswax. So maybe we could get customers for Mrs. Golden."

"Maybe we could!" cried Sue. "Let's tell the other boys and girls to get their fathers and mothers to let them buy things at Mrs. Golden's, and then she'll have a lot of customers!"

"Oh, let's!" cried Bunny Brown.

And they did. The next day, when Bunny and Sue were playing with Charlie, George, Mary, Sadie, Helen, Harry and Bobbie, the idea was spoken of again.

"Fellows and girls!" exclaimed Bunny, who got up to make a speech, "we have to help Mrs. Golden."

"You should speak of the girls first," said Sadie, who was a little older than the others.

"Well, anyhow, we ought to help Mrs. Golden," went on Bunny. "She needs customers. Now, if all of you would buy everything you could of her, like Sue and I do, maybe she wouldn't lose her store."

"My mother says she'd trade there if Mrs. Golden would deliver stuff," remarked Helen Newton. "But she says she can't cart heavy things from any store."

"My mother said the same thing," added Mary Watson.

"She can't afford to hire a delivery horse and wagon," said Charlie Star. "I know, 'cause I helped in her store."

"She needs an auto like Mr. Gordon," said Bobbie Boomer.

"Pooh, autos are only for big stores!" exclaimed Harry.

Bunny Brown seemed to be doing some hard thinking. He had a new idea.

"Fellows!" he suddenly cried, "I have it! I'll get a delivery wagon for Mrs. Golden!"

"You will?"

"A delivery wagon?"

"How?"

These cries greeted what Bunny had said.

"I'll take our Shetland pony, Toby, and deliver things for her in the little cart!" cried Bunny Brown. "If all of you will promise to buy as much as you can from her, I'll deliver things in our pony cart!"

"Hurray for the pony express!" cried Charlie Star. "I'll help!"

CHAPTER XXIV

BAD NEWS

The boys and girls, all of whom promised to buy as much as they could from Mrs. Golden and who also promised to tell their mothers at home that things could now be delivered from the little corner store, were bubbling over with fun and good-nature as they left the yard of Bunny and Sue where the "meeting" was held. But after his playmates had gone Bunny Brown began to do a little worrying.

"I know Toby will like to deliver groceries and be a pony express," said the little boy to his sister. "But maybe mother won't let us do it."

"Oh, I guess she will," said Sue.

"I'll ask her, anyhow," decided Bunny, and he did.

Mrs. Brown thought the matter over carefully when Bunny and Sue told her about it.

"Is Mrs. Golden really in such need of money?" asked Mrs. Brown.

"Oh, yes!" cried Bunny. "She feels so sad when Mr. Flynt comes and says he's going to close her store. And we'll feel sad if we don't have any place to go any more and learn how to work in it, Mother! Please let us take Toby and be a pony express!"

"I'll talk it over with your father," said Mrs. Brown.

The children waited anxiously for what their father should say, and they were glad when they heard him laugh after Mrs. Brown had spoken to him of the plan.

"Why, yes," he agreed. "I don't see any harm in it. Toby doesn't get enough exercise as it is. And Bunny and Sue can manage the little Shetland very well. The only thing is, I wouldn't want them to drive all over town delivering groceries—I mean out on the main street where there are so many autos now."

"Oh, we wouldn't go there!" promised Bunny.

"We might work it this way," went on Mr. Brown. "If there are things to be delivered on the other side of Main Street I'll let Bunker Blue do it. He can spare the time once a day. Bunny and Sue can do the rest of the delivery."

So it was decided, and you can imagine how delighted Bunny and Sue were when they hastened to tell the good news to Mrs. Golden.

"Why, that's perfectly wonderful!" exclaimed the old lady, and there were happy tears in her eyes. "Oh, you are two darling children to think so much of helping an old woman."

"You're not so old," declared Bunny politely. "Besides, we like to keep store; don't we, Sue?"

"Lots!" answered the little girl.

Bunny and Sue clerked in the store as much as they had time for, but as they were now to deliver things in the pony cart they could not spend so much time behind the counter. And Mr. Brown said that Bunny and Sue must both go in the pony cart, as it would be safer for them that way.

"Sue can hold Toby while you take the groceries into the houses," said Mr. Brown. "Only you mustn't lift too heavy boxes, Bunny."

"No, Daddy!" he promised. "If it's too heavy I'll lift it twice!" He meant he would make two trips of it.

Toby was almost as much help to Mrs. Golden as Bunny and Sue had been, for many housekeepers, when they found they could have groceries delivered from the corner store, took part of their trade there. And Bunny and Sue were quite proud to load up the basket cart with boxes and packages and start out to leave the orders at the different houses.

Mrs. Golden did not grow any younger or more active, and there were times when she could hardly get around the store. At such times, if Bunny and Sue had to be out with the pony cart, Charlie Star would come in and be a clerk.

When things needed to be delivered on the other side of Main Street, along which many automobiles were driven, then Bunker Blue was called on. He gladly drove the "pony express" as it was laughingly called, and many customers were served this way.

But in spite of this increase in trade the worried look did not leave Mrs. Golden's face, and, more than once, Bunny and Sue again saw her counting up her money and looking at bills she owed Mr. Flynt.

"Will you have to sell the place now?" asked Bunny one day, coming in with Sue to help tend store. The two previous days had been busy ones, when many customers had bought things.

"Well, I don't know about it, Bunny, my dear," was the answer. "More money is coming in, to be sure, but things cost so much I make hardly any profit. Things still look black. But don't worry. You and Sue are a big help. If Philip only gets that legacy, then I'll be all right!"

"I hope he does!" said Bunny Brown.

Several customers came in and the children helped Mrs. Golden wait on them. Then one woman wanted flour, sugar, and potatoes sent to her house on the other side of Main Street, a place where Bunny and Sue had never been.

"But we'll load the things in the pony cart," said Bunny to Sue, "and drive to our house. Bunker Blue is going to be there, for he's going to cut the grass, and he can drive across Main Street to Mrs. Larken's house."

"That will be all right," said Mrs. Golden. "It's very kind of you to help me this way."

The children started out with Toby, and they were almost at their own home when they heard a great shouting and racket behind them.

"Oh, Bunny!" cried Sue, "maybe we dropped something out of the cart and they're calling to us to pick it up."

Bunny gave one look back over the way they had come. Then he pulled hard on Toby's reins and shouted:

"No, we didn't drop anything, but here comes the fire engine!"

And, surely enough, dashing down the street was the shiny new engine that had lately been bought for Bellemere.

"Oh, pull over to one side!" cried Sue, clasping Bunny's arm. "Pull over to one side!"

"I—I'm trying to!" he answered. But Toby did not seem to want to go over near the curb, and out of danger. Once in a while the Shetland pony had a stubborn streak, and this was one of those times.

"Get over! Get over there!" cried Bunny, pulling on the reins.

But instead of swinging to the right Toby turned to the left, and down the street, clanging and thundering came the fire engine.

"Get out the way!"

"Look at those children!"

"Pull over! Pull over!" cried people along the sidewalk.

One or two men ran out to grasp the bridle of Toby and swing him over, for it seemed that all Bunny was doing had no effect. But before any of the men could reach the pony Bunker Blue came dashing along. He was on his way to the Brown house to cut the grass, and he saw the danger of Bunny and Sue.

"What's the matter with you, Toby? What's the matter?" cried Bunker Blue. The Shetland pony seemed to know the fish boy's voice, for he allowed himself to be swung over to the curb and out of danger just before the fire engine dashed by.

"Oh dear!" sighed Sue.

"Pooh! That wasn't anything!" declared Bunny Brown. "I could have got him over. And, anyhow, the fire engine would have steered out! But I'm glad you came, Bunker," he said, for this talk did not seem to show a kindly feeling toward the fish boy who had been so quick to act.

"Yes, I guess you'd 'a' been all right," said Bunker, with a laugh. "But that fire engine was going very fast. You've got to be careful of it."

And all the rush and excitement was for nothing, as there was no fire, the alarm being a false one. Bunker took charge of the pony cart and delivered the groceries before he cut the grass. Then Bunny and Sue drove back to the corner store.

They saw Mr. Flynt talking to Mrs. Golden as they entered.

"It's of no use!" the cross man was saying. "I have bad news for you. You'll have to give up the store, Mrs. Golden."

"Won't your company give me a little more time?" she asked.

"No," said Mr. Flynt. "We've been waiting and waiting, hoping you could pay. Of course things are better than early in the summer. I guess these children have helped you a lot," and he looked at Bunny and Sue. "But you don't take in enough money to pay your bills. If you could pay up you might get along, for you have a good trade now. But you can't pay your bills, and so we're going to sell you out!"

"Does that mean close up the store?" asked Bunny timidly.

"That's what it means, little man," was the answer, and Mr. Flynt did not seem so cross now. Perhaps he was sorry for what he had to do. "Mrs. Golden will have to give up her store."

CHAPTER XXV

GOOD NEWS

Bunny Brown and his sister Sue looked at each other with sad eyes. After all their work it had come to this. The store would be closed! They would have no place to come and have good times during the long vacation days! It was too bad! What was to be done?

Sue waited for Bunny to speak, as she usually did, and Bunny, after thinking the matter over, asked:

"Are you going to close it up right away?"

"Within a day or so, unless Mrs. Golden can pay her bills," answered Mr. Flynt. "We have waited as long as we can. I'm going to begin now to close out her business, but it will take two or three days. If she can raise the money in that time——"

"There's no use waiting or hoping—I can't do it!" sighed the old lady, with tears in her eyes. "I've tried my best, but I can't do it, even with the help of these dear children and the pony express," and she looked out of the window at Toby, hitched to the little basket cart.

"It is too bad," said Mr. Flynt. "We know you've done your best, and if you didn't owe so much you might get along now, with the start you have. But it takes all you can make to pay your back debts. It's best that you should give up the store. My company is sorry for you, but we've waited as long as we can. You'll have to sell out, Mrs. Golden."

"Yes, I suppose so," she agreed. "But if I could only hear from Philip, and if he could bring the money from that legacy, I could pay all I owe and start a bigger store. But I don't suppose there's any use hoping for that."

"No, I believe not," agreed Mr. Flynt. "Your son Philip doesn't seem to have gotten that legacy. Have you heard from him?"

"Not lately," said Mrs. Golden, with a sad shake of her head. "I don't know why he hasn't written. Perhaps because he has no good news for me."

"Very likely," said Mr. Flynt. "Well, I must go. You had better arrange to sell everything by the end of the week, and pay us what you can. We'll have to wait for the rest, I reckon."

"Won't there be a store here any more?" asked Sue.

"Oh, some one else may start one. It isn't a bad place for a grocery and notion shop," answered the black-whiskered man. "But Mrs. Golden can't keep this store any more."

"Maybe she can if my father will help her!" exclaimed Bunny. "He said he would!"

"Well, if some one would pay what she owes, of course she could keep on with the store," agreed Mr. Flynt. "But we can't wait any longer. We've got to sell her out."

When Bunny and Sue told at home that evening what had happened, Mrs. Brown said:

"Walter, can't you do something for that poor old woman?"

"Yes, I must try," he said. "I meant to look into her affairs long before this, but I've had so many other things to do that I let it go. We'll save the store for her if we can."

"'Cause we like to help tend it," said Bunny. "Don't we, Sue?"

"Yes," answered the little girl.

Instead of going to his boat and fish dock the next morning, as he nearly always did, Mr. Brown called to Bunny to get ready and go down to the corner grocery with him.

"May I come?" asked Sue.

"Yes," her father answered. "You are in this as much as Bunny. We are going to help Mrs. Golden if we can."

They found the old lady sitting sadly in her easy chair near the back of the store where she generally could be found when no customers needed to be waited on.

"Good morning, Mrs. Golden," said Mr. Brown. "I understand you are in trouble."

"If owing a lot of money and not being able to pay it is trouble, then I'm in almost up to my eyes," she answered, with a shake of her head.

"Like I was in the brook!" said Sue.

"Yes, I suppose so," sighed Mrs. Golden. "I'm afraid I've got to lose my store."

"Tell me how much you owe," begged Mr. Brown.

And when he heard he shook his head, saying:

"It is more than I thought. If it had been only about a hundred dollars I might have lent it to you, or found some one who would, but now I'm afraid nothing can be done."

"Do you mean the store will have to close?" asked Bunny.

"I'm afraid so, Son," replied his father.

"Oh dear!" sighed Mrs. Golden! "If Philip were only here then I might——"

"Well, here I am, Mother!" cried a voice at the front door. "What's the trouble?" and in came big, strong, jolly Philip Golden. He had just arrived on a train. "What's wrong?" he asked, for he could see that his mother had tears in her eyes.

The trouble was soon told.

"Sell the store!" he cried. "I guess not much! Didn't you get my telegram, Mother?"

"What telegram?"

"The one telling about the legacy. We have it—several thousand dollars! It won't make us rich, but it will be enough to make you comfortable for life. I heard the good news yesterday, and I sent you a telegram telling about it so you wouldn't worry any more."

"I never got your message!" said Mrs. Golden, smiling through her tears. "But it doesn't matter. I suppose there was some mistake and it went to the wrong address. But it was better to have you bring the good news. Are you sure we're to have the legacy?"

"Sure, Mother! I brought some money with me and more will come. You'll be all right now. You can pay all your bills and have plenty left over."

"Oh, I'm so glad!" cried Sue. "Then you can have a real nice store, can't you?"

"Yes," answered Mrs. Golden with a happy smile on her face, "I suppose I can. Oh, how glad I am, and how thankful I am to you dear children. You've helped me more than I can tell you."

"And we're going to help more!" cried Bunny Brown. "When you get your new store I'm going to be a clerk in it; can't I, Daddy?"

"Maybe," said Mr. Brown, with a smile.

And so the good news came after the bad, which is always the best way to have it come, I think. Mrs. Golden paid all her debts, and later she and her son Philip opened a larger store and did very well. Sometimes Bunny and Sue went to see the new place, but it was too far from their home for them to "work" in it. And, anyhow, there were other things for Bunny Brown and his sister Sue to do.

But now we have come to the end of our story and must say good-bye.

THE END

9 781836 573739